THE GHOSTS OF INISHFREE

AND

OTHER STORIES

BY

PATRICK CAMPBELL

The Ghosts of Inishfree
And
Other Stories

Published By P.H. Campbell
82 Bentley Ave
Jersey City, N.J. 07304

201 434 2432/ pathcampbe@aol.com

CONTENTS

INTRODUCTION

The stories in this book are not based on fiction, although some of the events described have been dramatized, and the names of some characters in these stories have been changed to protect the identities of those who have been portrayed.

There are no elements of fiction in *The Ghosts of Inishfree*, *The Idiot Savant, Stories about the Old Rectory, The Handprint on the Wall.* and *A Death In the Family.*

The location has been changed in *Barney Rua's Bar*, and fictional names have been given to the bar and the patrons of the bar. But the events described in this story are accurately portrayed.

The setting of the suicide story in *Ghosts* has been changed and fictional names given to the personalities in the story. But the description of the incident is accurate.

The setting and characters of *Maniac* has been changed, but the events occurred as described.

THANKS

The following people have provided assistance and their contribution is deeply appreciated.

Eileen Campbell, Jersey City, NJ

Anthony Bardon, Dublin.

Beattie Gallagher, Margaret Duffy, Maureen O'Sullivan, and Oscar Duffy, Burtonport, Co Donegal

Fonzie McCullough, Pat Boyle, Dennis Hanlon, Dungloe, Co.Donegal.

Mary Benoit, Connecticut

Ena O'Neill, Dublin.

OTHER BOOKS BY PATRICK CAMPBELL

A Molly Maguire Story

Memories of Dungloe

Death in Templecrone

The Last Days of Oscar Devanney

Tunnel Tigers

Who Killed Franklin Gowen

THE GHOSTS OF INISHFREE

My earliest memories of Inishfree Island, County Donegal, date back to a visit I made to the island with my father when I was nine years old. My father had gone to the island to attend a wake and he agreed to take me with him. During our approach to the island on a small sailboat, my father pointed out my grandfather's house, which was perched on high ground in the center of the island. It was a long, whitewashed one-story house that dominated the landscape.

We had a difficult time landing at the Scoilt Pier because time and time again a fast flowing current that careened right by the pier persisted in driving the boat offshore. Bur eventually, Paddy, the boatman, used a long pole with a hook at the end of it to grab an iron ring embedded in the concrete pier and pulled the boat towards the pier. Then my father jumped out of the boat and secured the boat to the ring with a sturdy rope.

During the maneuvers to get ashore, neither Paddy nor my father exhibited any signs of nervousness, and because of this, I did not feel too much afraid either. Paddy was an islander and must have been used to this exercise, and my father had been in and out of the island for decades so it was nothing unusual for him either. Still, the difficulty getting the boat tied up to the pier was a little unnerving.

*

I still remember the sights, sounds, and smells of the island that I experienced that day. As I walked across the pier I saw a huge pile of decaying seaweed six feet high that gave off a pungent odor. The odor was of salt mixed with decaying shellfish, and even though it was hardly a pleasant odor, I liked it and I would associate this odor with the island and all the pleasant memories I would have of this place in later years.

I was to learn afterwards that the seaweed had been harvested by my grandfather, Tim Gallagher, who was a fisherman and a gardener who used the seaweed to fertilize his potato and vegetable fields. He also sold seaweed as fertilizer to small farmers on the mainland.

A narrow sandy road meandered across the shoreline in the direction of half a dozen houses located near the beach, and then, just before it reached the houses, the road turned abruptly to the left and headed directly up a long incline towards my grandparents' home.

As we turned the corner and headed up the slope, my father noticed a man working in a field beside the road and called out to him. The man was Barney Gallagher; a first cousin of my mother, who was known on the island as Barney Paddy Bryan. Barney lived alone in a two-story house that was one of the two oldest houses on the island, each dating back to eighteenth century.

I cannot remember what Barney and my father talked about but it seemed that they talked for a long time, neither in any hurry to put an end to the conversation. And I do not know why I remember this encounter with Barney so well, because there was nothing dramatic about it, and it yet I can recall it as clearly as if it happened yesterday.

As Barney and my father talked I looked around and became aware of the persistent singing of one particular bird – a lark – that seemed to be serenading me from on high. I may have heard larks singing before, but if I had I had not been aware of it, and I was intrigued by the beauty and variety of the music coming from the heavens. In the years that followed, I would think of Inishfree whenever I heard a lark sing, even if I was a hundred miles from the island.

The fields and little hillocks on each side of the road on the way up to Tim's house offered other distractions that kept me interested as I waited for Barney and my father to end their conversation. Among these distractions was a riot of wildflowers that carpeted the areas not cultivated with corn, potatoes and vegetables, and these wildflowers attracted platoons of butterflies and bumble bees, who competed with one another for the choicest flowers.

All this activity was probably ignored by the islanders but was fascinating to a small boy like me who was being raised in a very big house in the village of Dungloe and whose exposure to larks, butterflies, and bumblebees was limited.

Eventually my father ended his conversation with Barney and we continued our way up the sandy lane towards my grandfather's house. When we were half way up the lane I noticed a huge boulder, about ten feet high, in a field near the road. The boulder was shaped like a pear and it was balanced precariously on the narrow stem-like part of the boulder.

My father saw me staring at the boulder and he said: "Your Uncle James thinks that fairies come out from under that boulder at night and dance around the island until dawn."

I don't recall making any response to this, possibly because I did not know what to say. I thought fairies were confined to the children's books I had out in Dungloe and I had no idea they were running around Inishfree at night.

I also didn't know whether these fairy frolics were good or bad. But my father did not seem to be scared of the idea, so I wasn't scared either. Still, I was just a little uneasy at the idea that these supernatural beings had a habitat so close to my grandparents' cottage. I wondered if they ever danced around my grandfather's house at night.

Eventually we arrived at the house and were m welcomed by my grandparents and my uncle James, who was also there that day.

My grandmother was dressed in along black dress that went all the way to her ankles and she had a black scarf covering her head. She was over eighty and looked very old. My grandfather wore a woolen pullover and woolen pants and old wellington boots and he too was over eighty and looked very old. Uncle James was not as wrinkled and stooped as the other two but he also looked old.

I had seen all three of them many times before out in Dungloe in my parents' house, but they had looked very different then because they had been dressed up in their Sunday best and I was very impressed by them. Somehow the fancy clothes had made me overlook their wrinkled faces.

I took an immediate liking to the house, however, and I don't know the reason for this because it was a Spartan place. I think it was the atmosphere that I liked because it seemed to welcome you and make you feel at home.

The house was nothing to brag about: it consisted of two bedrooms, a big living room, and a tiny kitchen and pantry. One bedroom had plain whitewashed walls, a large wardrobe, two beds, and had a large picture of the Sacred Heart on one wall. A carpet of linoleum covered the floor.

The other bedroom was much fancier: it had a large brass bed, carpet on the floor, many pictures on the wall, and several pieces of nice-looking furniture. It also had a small fireplace set in the wall made of cast iron.

This small house used to be home to a family of nine: my grandparents and their children, Patrick, Barney, John, James, Mary, Bridget, and Annie. All were gone except James, who had inherited the chore of taking care of his parents.

The living room had a dining table and six chairs, several benches, set around the walls, and a wooden bed pushed against the wall near the fireplace, all hand made. A hand-made colorful woolen quilt covered the bed.

The entire inside and outside of the house was whitewashed with a lime that my grandfather had made from crushed seashells. Grandpa had gathered thousands of the shells and heated them in a lime kiln until they turned into a white powder that could be used to whitewash the inside and outside of the house.

The open fireplace was the focal point of the room and a large cheerful fire was burning there, even though it was in the middle of summer, and a steaming black iron kettle hung from a hook suspended above the fire.

My grandmother made tea and served my father and me large slices of home made bread with raisins in it, and one large boiled egg for me and two eggs for my father. The eggs had come from the chickens that were running around outside the house. She also offered us home made butter and home made blackberry jam. I thought the jam was delicious, but I thought the butter, churned by my grandmother from cream that came from one of her cows, had a funny taste – very salty and not at all like the sweet creamery butter that I was used to in Dungloe. However, I ate it anyway because I was hungry and because I was afraid I might insult my grandmother, who I heard was very easily insulted.

Over the years however I grew to love my grandmother's butter and always preferred it to the "store" butter I got in Dungloe. I also acquired a taste for my grandmother's buttermilk and her currant bread, which I thought was the best bread in the world.

After the meal was consumed my father said he was going to pay his respects to the bereaved family, who lived half a mile away, and that he would see me the following morning, as he intended to sit up all night with the corpse, a common practice in northwest Donegal.

He did not invite me to go along with him to the wake and if he did I would not have gone with him as I was petrified of corpses.

Three years prior to that, when I was six, there had been an automobile accident outside our door in Dungloe, and one of the victims of the accident had been killed and had been carried into our kitchen and laid out on the floor while efforts were made to revive him.

I was present during the entire event and at one time I was left alone with the corpse – he motionless on the floor; I, motionless on a couch, afraid to move.

At that time, I had little conception of death but instinctively I knew that death was a very serious state of affairs because it always led to a burial in a hole in the ground. Afterwards, I did not want to go to the Church on Sunday because we had to walk through the graveyard to the front door of the Church, and my sister Rose told me that there were several dead bodies lying beneath every tombstone -- an idea that terrified me since there appeared to be a multitude of tombstones in the graveyard. Rose, who liked to tease me, told me there were more dead people in Dungloe than living people, and sometimes these dead people came out and walked around the streets after midnight.

I had been afraid of corpses since then, and would never visit one of my own free will.

When my father left, my grandmother told me that I would be sleeping down in the lower room with Uncle James.

"We sleep there," she said pointing to the bed by the fireplace.

I thought of the fancy room on the other side of the living room and asked my grandmother who was going to sleep there. She turned away from me and did not answer me, and when I was about to ask her the question again a warning look from Uncle James made me hold my tongue.

Later, James told me that the room had been my Auntie Annie's room. Auntie Annie had contracted tuberculosis in America and had come home to die five years previously. She had died six months after her arrival and it had broken Granny's heart and she could not bear to talk about her.

Granny had kept the room exactly as it was when Annie was alive and no one was allowed to sleep there, even if the house was crowded.

After an awkward period of silence Grandpa told me to go out and visit the chickens, the donkey and the cows, an activity that kept me amused for more than an hour.

The chickens were very tame and two of them even let me pet them, but the donkey and the cows treated me with indifference and seemed bored by my attempts to make friends with them.

From my high vantage point I could see all of the island and the wide band of sea that surrounded it. I could also see Dungloe off in the distance, at the head of Dungloe Bay, a large cluster of houses nestled up against the hills.

I could not see any people from this great distance, but I could see movement on the roads leading into Dungloe and I assumed that I was looking at cars coming and going from the town.

I wondered what my mother was doing in our house out in the village at that particular moment.

Two years previously, an older boy who lived next door to me had received a telescope from Santa and one day he loaned it to me so that I could look in at Inishfree. My father set up the telescope for me and focused it on my grandfather's house, which could be seen because it occupied the highest point in the island.

When he showed me how to focus the lens so I saw the house clearly I was utterly amazed to see my grandmother walk out the door with a bucket in her hand and dip it into a huge cement tank at the gable of the house. I told my father about what I was seeing and after peering into the lens he said Granny was getting a bucket of rainwater since there was no running water in the house.

Ever since that day I wanted to go into Inishfree and see the house, but my parents would not let me because they said that ever since Auntie Annie died Granny would not let any of the grandchildren visit, and the only time we saw her was when she came out to Dungloe, which was a very rare occurrence.

However, I kept begging my parents for years to bring me in anyway, and eventually my father decided to bring me with him when he was going in to the wake and he took the risk of annoying Granny. My father was nervous about what she might say, but she said nothing and was very polite to me and so was my grandfather. I got no hugs, of course, because neither of them was into hugging. Neither were my parents for that matter: I don't recall ever getting a hug from either one of them, but I never thought this was strange since most if not all of my friends went without hugs also.

As I peered out at Dungloe in the distance, I wished I had a telescope so I could spy on the village the way I had spied on Inishfree years before.

I looked all around the island and I could see that the islanders who were not at the wake were busy in the fields.

Each of the islanders had plots of land ranging from twelve to twenty five acres, some of it bog land, and some of it in carefully cultivated fields. Inishfree was comprised of 641 acres in all and it was very rough terrain, full of boulders, little glens, bogs with sheets of rock jutting out of them, and, of course the fields that had been carefully won over from this wilderness.

When the first settlers came from the mainland to the island centuries ago, the island was covered with a carpet of bog with boulders and rocks jutting out of it. The first settlers picked level stretches of bog and carefully drained the water-logged soil, and then they fertilized the soil with seaweed harvested from the shore. After that they planted potatoes, corn and a variety of vegetables which thrived in the newly claimed fertile land.

As more settlers moved in most of the island that could be reclaimed was reclaimed and by the 1850s there were 42 homesteads on the island.

The island men grew all the vegetables their families needed. They harvested peat from the bogs and stacked it neatly beside their homes, providing a yearlong supply of fuel for the fire. In addition, in the waters around Inishfree, they harvested lobster, salmon, and cod as cash crops; and they harvested herring, mackerel, whiting, and other fish for their annual supply of protein.

Nobody ever went hungry in Inishfree. Some islanders might have a problem with loneliness, and a few might have a problem with alcohol, but everyone had an abundance of food while I was growing up, and they had warm cozy houses that sheltered them from the cold winds of winter.

My grandmother had a large barrel in the pantry full of salted fish that had been captured from the sea by James and my grandfather.

Out in a field behind the house my grandfather had a deep pit in which he stored potatoes, turnips, carrots and other vegetables that he grew in the large field below the house. My grandfather not only kept the household supplied with vegetables, but he was able to feed the cows, the donkey and the chickens as well.

In addition, he had always had vegetables left over that he sold for cash in Dungloe. With the cash, my grandmother bought the tea, sugar and flour that could not be produced on the island.

Inishfree was a self-supporting little community of 30 homes in the 1940s, down from the 40 homes in the 1840s, and the population consisted of several hundred people who could provide for themselves, and who supported each other in time of need.

On my first afternoon on Inishfree, we all sat down to a typical island meal: salted herring, boiled potatoes and cabbage. I had a big struggle with the salted herring, because I was used to sweet fresh herring covered in butter and lightly salted, and this fish was bitter on the palate. But I soldiered on because the other three people were eating up the herring as if it was ice cream, and I did not want to appear contrary by complaining.

However, I was glad when the last morsel went down my throat and I drank a big glass of water afterwards to wash away the taste.

After the meal, we had a visitor: Winnie Duffy, who was my father's first cousin. She lived in a big house down by the beach. My father pointed it out to me on the way up.

Winnie had been at the wake and she had found out from my father that I was up in Tim's house, so she decided to invite me down to play with her two sons, who were my own age.

My grandmother seemed a little reluctant to let me go, but Winnie persisted and soon I was on my way down to the beach and the beginning of a long relationship with the Duffy brothers, who gave me one more reason in the years ahead to return to Inishfree.

"Be back before dark", were my grandmothers parting words, to which James added: "If you come up after dark the fairies that live under the big rock will be out and they will kidnap you".

I did not know whether or not I should believe him. But I certainly knew I would be back up the road before dark, since I saw no point in taking a chance with beings who might very well exist, and who also might not be that friendly to someone like me who had just blown in from Dungloe, a place far removed from this isolated community.

As I passed the boulder on the way down the road my pace quickened and I walked far ahead of Winnie.

When she caught up with me Winnie said: "It looks like James has been telling you about the fairies."

I did not respond, and she said nothing more about it. But I wondered why she did not tell me there were no fairies … if there were no fairies under the big rock. Her silence was unsettling.

The afternoon and evening with the Duffy brothers sealed my love affair with Inishfree because I had adventures with them that I could never have had out in Dungloe.

First, there was the beach that was a few yards from Winnie's door, which was covered in soft white sand.

The beach also had an abundance of colorful and exotic shells. This beach was very different from the silt covered beach at Dungloe that was a foot deep in places with the mud the Dungloe River had brought down from the mountains.

The estuary of the Dungloe River was also covered by all kinds of debris tossed into the river upstream, and even though people did bath in the area during the summer, anyone who wanted to visit a clean sandy beach had to travel six miles to Arlands at the north of Dungloe or six miles to Maghery on the west. So, the Inishfree beach seemed a great luxury to me, and I was amazed the Duffy brothers did not seem to be impressed by it and were puzzled by my enthusiasm.

It was high tide when I first went down the lane with Winnie and the sea had come right up to within seven feet of the Duffy house.

But then it slowly ebbed out revealing the glorious beach and all the marine life stranded by the ebbing waters.

When the sea had ebbed out almost a mile it left behind large puddles of water in the uneven beach, and in these puddles were a host of little crabs that scuttled around trying to find somewhere to hide.

There were also cockles and winkles in these pools and Patsy and Joe Duffy gathered them up in a bucket they had brought along with them. They told me these shellfish made great soup and they were also delicious to eat. The boys would not bother with the crabs because they were too small, and the only crabs they ate were the huge crabs caught in their father's nets when he was out fishing.

The claws of these large crabs were roasted on the open fire and I can still remember the first time that I had tasted one in the Duffy house years later. It was absolutely delicious.

Our safari across the beach brought us to a huge pool, several hundred yards long and a foot deep. The pool lay between Inishfree and a smaller island named Innishunny that could be reached at low tide and was used by the Inishfree people to graze their cattle. Nobody lived there.

Joe had brought along a pitchfork which he said he used to catch fluke that had been stranded by the ebbing tide. We walked beside the pool and then Patsy told us to be quiet, so we stood still and gazed into the pool. I could see nothing in the crystal-clear water.

"The fluke are flat fish that are the same color as the sand and you can only see them when they move," Joe said. "When they move they kick up clouds of sand"

We stood there for several minutes without seeing anything, and then Patsy picked up a pebble and tossed it into the pool, and immediately two lines of sand streaked across the pool and ended abruptly as the fish wiggled their way once again into the soft white sand.

"You keep your eye on that one, and I will get the other one over there," said Joe to Patsy.

Joe carefully padded around the pool until he was close to where the fluke was hiding, and then with an expert thrust of the pitchfork he impaled the large fluke and dragged it up onto the sand, an operation that was difficult because the fluke kept flailing wildly in the water.

Joe managed to subdue the fluke but the ruckus created by the catch made the second fluke break cover and disappear. Despite searching for an hour we could not locate him, and we even waded into the water and kicked around with our feet, but the fluke, who must have had some degree of intelligence, refused to leave his hiding place. In the end, we gave up, and allowed the fluke to live for another day.

Our last stop of the day was a visit to Innishunny where there was a Fairy Ring that the boys said was sacred to the fairies. They said the fairies came out at night and danced around the ring until dawn.

I wasn't sure what a fairy ring was until I saw this perfect ring of dark green grass set in a field of lighter green grass at the edge of the island. Around the ring there were a number of foot-high weeds with yellow flowers that Joe called gushigans.

"At night these gushigans turn into fairy horses and when the fairies get tired dancing they get up on these horses and gallop around the ring for hours. They love doing that. You must never pull one of these gushigans out of the ground, because if you do the fairies will take a terrible revenge. They will turn you into a fluke like the one I caught and then everyone will be trying to stick a pitchfork in you."

It didn't occur to me to ask Joe how he knew all this, but he probably would have an explanation if I asked him.

I told myself that Joe was just making fun of me, but I never pulled up a gushigan in the fairy ring in all the years that followed. I was determined not to take any chances.

After we visited the fairy ring it was tea time and we all trouped up to Winnie's house, tired and hungry from our adventure. Winnie had a little banquet ready that consisted of pancakes, strawberry jam, and boiled eggs. This was the second time I had eggs that day, but I did not mind because I liked eggs. We were joined at the meal by Pat Roddy Duffy, Winnie's husband, and James, Winnie's brother.

The two men spoke very little to one another, but James and Winnie chatted away for most of the evening. At one point, James asked me if I had seen the white horse in on Innishunny, and I said I did not see any white horse at all.

"You were lucky, "said James. "He is a fairy stallion that does not like strangers."

"If you were foolish enough to get up on his back he would have galloped up into the clouds and you would have wound up in Tir Na nOg for the rest of your life. I suppose he didn't bother with you because the boys were with you."

I looked at the boys, but they were busy eating and if they heard James they did not respond in any way. I looked at Winnie and Pat Roddy, but they were also busy chomping away and I got no reaction from them either.

But I decided to believe in the fairies and their horses, because I wanted to believe in them, and I wanted to believe in them because their presence in Inishfree made this island a very strange and wonderful place, almost like a secret other-world that made Dungloe look like a boring drab place where nothing exciting ever happened. I made up my mind there and then that I was going to come into this island every chance I got.

We sat by the fire after tea time, and James told a few ghost stories that added more flavor to the island.

He said that on every 10th of July at midnight, a man walked out of the sea and patrolled around the island all night.

James said he believed the man was the ghost of a fisherman who was drowned a hundred years before and he came back every year on the anniversary of the drowning to look for his relatives.

"They are all dead," said James, "But he doesn't seem to know this, or even know that he is dead himself."

I asked James if he had ever seen the man, and he seemed shocked by the question, as if I had said something that was completely outrageous.

"I would never go out after midnight on July 10th -- nobody in their right mind would. We all stay in behind locked doors. About forty years ago there was an islander who got drunk and went out to see the ghost and he was found dead himself the following morning. Some people say that man now patrols the island with the other ghost."

James had many more stories to tell and the evening flew in until it began to get late and darkness was approaching. So, I said good bye and headed off up the road in the gathering darkness. I quickened my pace as I passed the big boulder, but I did not see any fairies, although I looked over my shoulder every minute until I got up to the house, and I was very glad to get in the door unharmed.

Granny was sitting at the fireplace putting the fire to bed for the night by covering the glowing embers with ashes, which insulated the embers and preserved them until the fire could be revived again in the morning.

Granny said my father had come around to see how I was, and she told him I was playing with the Duffy boys down on the beach. She then told me to go to bed, but not to make any noise because James had to get up at three in the morning to go fishing.

I went down to the lower bedroom and crept in beside Uncle James in the soft feather bed made from a mattress stuffed with the feathers of deceased chickens. An eiderdown, also stuffed with feathers served as a blanket.

I was going to roll over and go to sleep, but then James, who was not asleep at all, began to talk to me and tell me more stories about the island that was even scarier than the ones Winnie's brother had told me.

"Whatever you do," he said, "don't go near that big crowd of boulders that are over near our bog, because that is where the island banshee lives. You are safe enough during the day, but don't go over there when it is getting dark, because they say that she is liable to come out of her den and anyone who sees her goes blind."

Of course, with a warning like that there was little chance I would go near those boulders day or night.

Uncle James said there was another clump of boulders on the west side of the island that I should also stay away from. "That's where the black hound has his den."

He went on to say that the black hound was, like the banshee, a foreteller of death, and he sometimes appeared near the house of a dying islander, as an omen that death was near. "My mother said the black dog was outside the house the night Annie died, and when my mother saw it she knew the end was near."

I asked him about the difference between the banshee and the black hound and he said the banshee cried out a warning of death, but did not visit the house, whereas the black hound never uttered a sound.

I do not know when James got up to go fishing; I only know that when I woke up at 8am he was gone. James and two other islanders were the crew of a small sailing boat that went to sea for eighteen hours at a time fishing for salmon, lobster, herring, cod, or whatever other fish were in season. They carried with them a score of lobster pots and several nets and they went to sea in all types of weather. They sold most of their catch in Burtonport and only brought fish home if Granny's fish barrel was becoming empty.

My father told me once that sea fishing on a small sailing boat was brutal and dangerous work and that I was never to think of it as exciting. He told me this because he knew I loved to go out fishing with him on the lakes and rivers around Dungloe and I loved everything about the activity: the small rowing boat, the casting of our lines, and the excitement when we caught fish.

"Your Uncle James has to go out there when it is bitterly cold and when the high seas toss the boat around, and at the end of the night they might come home with no fish at all to show for eighteen hours work because the nets were destroyed by the storm. James earns every penny he gets."

My grandfather also fished but he fished with a small rowing boat in the quiet bays that were sheltered from the Atlantic by the string of islands off the coast. Grandpa was too old to fish out at sea alone, and too contrary to fish with anyone else, but he was able to harvest some fish in the quiet bays and plenty of mussels and winkles from the strands around the islands and he was able to turn this fish and shellfish into cash. When he went out to Burtonport with his catch, Granny sent a shopping list with him, and he turned the cash into flour, tea, tobacco and other items. If there was money left over he brought it back to Granny, who served as director of finance in the Gallagher household.

After a breakfast that consisted of a large cup of tea and a bowl of oatmeal porridge that was covered in homemade butter, milk, and sugar, and a large slice of home made soda bread, Granny sent me out to the henhouse to gather up the eggs that the hens had laid during the night. She gave me a basket to carry the eggs in.

The henhouse had rows of shelving erected against the wall, and grandpa had built a dozen nests made of hay on each shelf, and each of the hens claimed one of these nests as it's own. I found eighteen eggs in all, and after counting the chickens out in the yard and getting a count of thirty-six, I concluded that half of the chickens were not laying eggs.

But just to be sure, I checked all the nests carefully once more, and came up with the same count.

When I reported this to Granny, she said that a dozen of the hens were not laying at the moment, so that would explain the shortage of a dozen eggs. "But some of those chickens must be getting ready to become mothers, and when they are that way they find a hiding place to lay the eggs in, and then they go and sit on them so the eggs hatch into little chickens."

Granny then decided to search around the fields near the house looking for the secret nests, and eventually she found one with three eggs. But she did not take the eggs, because she said she wanted to keep a close eye on the nests to see which chicken had laid the eggs there.

"When I find out which chicken owns the eggs, I will pick a dozen big eggs and put them on a special nest in the big barn, and then I will add the eggs the chicken laid to them.

"When the chicken goes looking for her eggs, she will find them with the other dozen and she will think she laid them all herself and sit down and hatch the whole gang of them. It is easy to fool some chickens. Most of them never know that all the eggs they are sitting on are not their own. Of course every now and then you will see a smart chicken that knows its own eggs and a chicken like that will kick other eggs out of the nest. You can't fool them at all."

Granny went on to tell me that one of the chickens in her brood was very sneaky, because she would disappear for two weeks and then would appear with a dozen chicks in tow. "I have never been able to find out where she goes, but it must be far away, because I have searched high and low for her nest but have never been able to find it."

She then pointed out the culprit, who was a small innocent-looking red-feathered chicken who did not look sneaky at all.

A little while later Grandpa asked me to go with him to the bog to bring back two baskets of peat for the fire. Grandpa put a harness on the donkey and then attached the baskets to the harness; one on each side of the donkey's belly.

Then, off we went to the bog that was five hundred yards from the back of the house. I had seen these baskets used in Dungloe before, they were called creedles out there, and I had seen men carry them on their backs as they brought the peat out of the bogs to the main road, where it could be brought home on a pony and cart, or on a lorry. However, there were no ponies, or carts, or lorries in Inishfree, only donkeys and these donkeys were used to bring the peat from the bog directly to the house, which in a way was very convenient.

As we headed out towards the bog, my grandfather told me that my grandmother would not mind if I came in and stayed with them for my summer holidays.

He said Granny could see I had a great time on the island the day before, and he said Granny seemed fond of me and didn't mind having me around.

"But don't let on that I told you, because she would not like that at all. Everything is very hush hush with your granny and she can't stand people who carry stories."

Grandpa said that this was the first time since Annie died that Granny had let any young people come around the house, so this was a very big thing for her.

"But if you do come in, you must do a lot of jobs around the house before you go down to visit the Duffy boys. When your brothers and sisters came in here to stay all of them had jobs to do every day, and there was no such thing as looking at the house as a free hotel. Your job will be to help me weed the vegetable gardens, and to bring the peat home with the donkey, and you will do it by yourself, because I will teach you how to work the donkey today. You will also help James mend his lobster pots and nets, but you won't have to do anything inside the house as housework is women's work. Do you agree to this?"

I was only too happy to agree and I asked if I could stay here and not go back to Dungloe when my father came back from the wake, but he said he could not let me do that, because I had to ask my mother's permission first.

"Women want to be the boss," he said. "And they can get very contrary if you do not get their permission first."

I did not mind the idea of working for my keep, since I had a great many chores to do every day out in Dungloe, including bringing peat in from the peat shed, helping my father weed the garden, and running to the shops for groceries. Besides Joe and Patsy Duffy had told me that they, too, had to work every day, and had only got the day off because I was around.

When my father came back early in the afternoon, Granny told him I could spend my holidays in the island if was alright with my mother. My father seemed very surprised by the offer, but he said he would bring the matter up with my mother when we got home.

"You know, this is the busy time of the year for us out in Dungloe and his mother will be counting on his help."

We had a small hotel and restaurant business in Dungloe and the summer was always a busy time.

But I did not want to hear any talk like that because I knew that each of my two brothers and five sisters had spent their summers in Inishfree when they were growing up, and I thought it would be very unfair if I were the only one to lose out on the experience, now that Granny was in the mood to allow grandchildren into the island once again.

I did not say anything to my father but I was determined to have a big argument with my mother if she did not let me return to the island, no matter what her reason.

*

After we said goodbye to my grandparents, my father said that he would take me on a walk around the parts of the island I had not seen before we headed back to the pier and the boat that would bring us out to Dungloe.

"We have two hours before we leave," he said. "This should be plenty of time to show you everything that there is to see. I was delighted at the opportunity and went along with him eagerly.

We came down the road from Tim's house and then turned left at an intersection. If we had gone right we would have come to the school house, and if we had gone straight ahead we would have wound up at the beach.

After several hundred yards, we turned left again and headed up an incline until we were on the same level as Tim's only five hundred yards further west.

On this road, we had a clear view of the west coast of the island and the string of other islands further out in the bay.

My father halted for a moment and began to describe to me the family relationship we had with some of the other islands.

"Your grandfather Tim was born on Aranmore, that big island that looks like a mountain out behind Winnie's house. Tim was born in 1850, just after the great famine of the 1840s. The family lived up there on the top north corner of the island near the edge of the cliffs. His grandfather, Patrick Gallagher, had a great view of the sea right up to Bloody Foreland, 12 miles to the northeast. In the great naval battle between the English and the French that was fought between Aranmore and Bloody Foreland in 1798 the whole family had a ringside seat for the battle. The French, who were bringing an army in to help the Irish, who were rebelling against the English, lost the battle, and Wolfe Tone, the Irish leader who was on a French ship, was captured and sentenced to death. Did they tell you anything about all this at school yet?"

I said we learned a little bit about the Rebellion of 1798, but nobody said a word about Patrick Gallagher, or his view of the famous battle.

My father went on to say that Tim's grandfather also met Napper Tandy, another famous Irish leader of the 1798 Rebellion who had landed in nearby Burtonport with a boat load of arms to give to Irish rebels. He said I should ask Tim to tell me all about the 1798 Rebellion as Tim was a great storyteller.

I told my father that I would ask Tim about the Rebellion, but in my heart I knew I would not bother, because I cared nothing for those ancient battles. History lessons are wasted on the very young because I thought at this time in my life that history was very boring.

I decided to be truthful with my father and I told him that I was far more interested in events that were taking place on the island in the present – events like the fairies that were running around the island at night and the Black Dog and the Banshee who were holed up in dens on the island. I told him Uncle James had told me all about them.

My father did not answer me for a while and then he said that my Granny had said the black hound visited the house the night Annie died. He also said his brother Owen said he had heard a banshee cry the night that their father had died. But my father said that he had never seen a black hound or heard a banshee, and it was time for me to worry about hounds or banshees when I saw or heard them myself. Until that time came I should put them out of my mind. This was easier said than done.

I brought up the fairies next. I told him about the fairy ring I had seen on Innishunny and the stories Uncle James had told me about the fairies living under the big boulder down the road, and he smiled and said: "They are really making sure that you will not wander around the island at night."

Then he went on to say that he had never met the fairies who lived under the great boulder, and all he knew about the boulder was that it had been sitting there for ten thousand years. He said a professor from Dublin who once visited the island said the boulder was dumped there during the Ice Age, and that there was another one like it over in Crolly ten miles away in the mountains. He said that movement of glaciers during the Ice Age carved out all the glens in the area and deposited huge boulders all over the place. He asked me if I they had told me about the Ice Age in school and I said they had not got around to it yet.

I did not ask him any questions about the Ice Age because I did not want another long history lesson. My father was a lot like my grandfather Tim, he was a great storyteller who would tell you stories even if you did not want to hear them. I had asked my father about the fairies and he had told me about the Ice Age.

But then he surprised me by telling me a story about the fairy ring on Innishunny. He said that before he married my mother he had come in to visit his Aunt Nappy, who was Winnie's mother. He had brought his brother Owen in with him, and while they were there he had pulled a gushigan from the fairy ring. It had been a bright summer's day up until that point, but then a fierce storm rolled over Aranmore and pounded the island for days.

"We had only planned to stay on the island for the day, but we were stranded here for several days, because the seas were too rough to go out. But a good thing came out of all this, because I visited Tim's while I was stranded and met your mother, and shortly after that we were married."

"Did you blame the fairies for the storm?" I asked him.

"Your Uncle Owen blamed them, but I always looked on the bright side: I got a wife and eight children from the storm. You wouldn't be standing here today if it weren't for the storm."

His answer was unsatisfactory -- he had dodged the question of fairy responsibility. My father was like that: he could be hard to pin down on a question he did not want to answer.

Ahead of us was a cluster of several cottages and outside of these cottages were a number of people working on various chores.

There were men out in the bogs working on harvesting the peat; other men were out in the fields harvesting the hay, while others tended to vegetable gardens. And there were a number of young people down on the shore, most older than me. Inishfree seemed like a very lively place and everyone seemed to spend their time outdoors.

We had walked over to the south end of the island by this time, and my father changed the subject, just as we arrived at an aged tree stump that stuck out of the bog.

"Do you see this here, this wood has been here for six thousand years?"

I looked at the weather-beaten stump, unimpressed.

"There are stumps like that all over the island that have been there since the ancient times when the island and the mainland was covered with trees."

I liked the idea of Inishfree covered with trees. There were no woodlands in northwest Donegal during this time, just bogs and boulders, and I would have liked woodlands because I could have plenty of hiding places to play cowboys and Indians with my friends.

My father continued with the tour, pointing out places that were of interest to him, though not necessarily of interest to me.

"Two of my grand aunts married into those houses in the 1820s", pointing to two small cottages by the beach.

"They were Sweeney sisters from Meenmore. They were the aunts of Winnie's mother. My aunt, Rose Campbell, married a man named O'Donnell and lived there," pointing to another small cottage.

He then turned his attention to the mainland, which was just a mile or so across the sea at this point. "Over there is Termon and there used to be a saint living there a thousand years or so ago"

"She had a convent there until the Vikings came and wrecked it. Have they told you in school about the Vikings? Real rascals, they were. And see that headland over there on the mainland with that tower on the top? That is called a Martello Tower and was set up there by the British after the Seventeen Ninety Eight Rebellion and was used to watch the ocean so the French Navy did not sneak up on them again. And out there in the ocean is a small island named Ilancrone, where Tim has a shack that he used to shelter in if the seas got very rough when he was out fishing. He doesn't go out there anymore because he is too old."

We continued around the island as my father gave a detailed description of our family relationship to some of the houses, and described the historic ruins that could be seen on the mainland and on neighboring islands. My father was obviously deeply interested in the history of this whole area, but I was nine years old and I had no interest at all in it and would only develop an interest in the subject when he was long gone.

Eventually we came to the schoolhouse, which was closed for the summer. "Your older brothers and sisters attended school here when your mother sent them in here during the winter and spring." I had never been sent in here to school and I wondered why my mother had banished the others for months at a time. Then we took a short cut from the school to the Scoilt Pier and the boat that was waiting to bring us out to Dungloe.

I was not at all happy about the idea of returning to Dungloe. I would have preferred to remain in Inishfree. Only a day had passed since I had landed on the island, but it seemed more like a long exciting lifetime and I was very eager to come back again as soon as possible.

As we sailed away from the pier, I looked back at the island bathed in sunshine, and I wondered why my mother had ever left this beautiful place. It did not seem to make any sense to me.

*

I expected a great deal of resistance from my mother when I told her I wanted to go into Inishfree for the rest of the summer, and I stressed the fact that I had been invited by Granny to bolster my argument. However, I received no opposition at all and I was told that I could go in anytime I found someone to take me in.

I went off to Inishfree the following day and began what was to become an annual summer pilgrimage to the island for the next five years.

During this time I got to know everyone who lived on the island and had been in every house at least once. My closest associates among the younger people was Joe and Patsy Duffy, Gerard O'Donnell, James Doherty, who was several years older than me, and Donal O'Sullivan, who was four years younger.

My affection for the island never wavered, and every year I would look forward to a summer of fishing and swimming on the island beaches, and at the end of every summer, I would get depressed at the thought of returning to Dungloe.

But, during the last Summer I spent in Inishfree my relationship with the island underwent a dramatic change.

My grandfather had become ill and spent most of his time in bed, and I could see that my grandmother wanted to devote all her time to taking care of him and had little time to devote to me. She did not complain to me but I could see that her entire focus was on her bed-ridden husband.

I knew I was becoming an intrusion, just as my brothers and sisters had when Auntie Annie was sick. My mother was aware of this and told me I had to come home ... so I did.

Later on in the year, my Inishfree friend Gerard O'Donnell died suddenly of a ruptured appendicitis, and the shock of his death was a very traumatic experience for me.

Finally, there was the drowning of an island youth near the pier at Scoilt, and it seemed to me that one tragedy after another was happening on the island.

My mother then told me that even if my grandfather regained his health I could not spend the summers on Inishfree anymore because I was needed at home. My brother Bernie had already left home to join the American navy, and my sister Rose had left to work in a hotel in Edinburgh, and I was the last and youngest member of the family who would be at home during the summers.

So, my love affair with my summers in Inishfree came to an abrupt end when I was fourteen years old and would never be resumed again. I deeply regretted the change that this brought to my life, because it eliminated the one thing that made the long winters in Dungloe bearable: the knowledge that when summer came around again I would be as free as one of those larks who wandered the skies over the island.

Although I did not know it at the time life on the island was about to undergo changes that would put an end to an island culture that had existed for almost 150 years. These changes did not happen overnight but occurred over a period of twenty years, but when these changes were complete Inishfree was no longer the island that I loved so dearly as a boy.

I was not aware of the gradual changes at first because changes taking place in my own life got all my attention.

When I was fourteen, I was sent off to a secondary school in Letterkenny, 40 miles away, because there was no secondary school in Dungloe.

I was away for most of the year and when I returned in the Summer I had to work all day, every day in our hotel. Sometimes I would go out into our back garden and look across the bay at Inishfree and wonder what was going on in the island at that particular moment, but I did not visit the island because Granny was nursing her bed-ridden husband and could not cope with young visitors.

I knew however that changes were taking place in the Inishfree. Donal Sullivan had gone off to work in Scotland when he was fifteen, and the Duffy Brothers followed shortly afterwards. There were deaths on the island and I watched the coffins coming out on the boats. And I was aware that the population was declining because few babies were being born there and the older people who died were not being replaced.

I did not know the reason for this gradual and ominous change to the vitality of the island, but I sensed that somehow the island was in terminal decline for reasons that I could not comprehend. Life had remained unchanged in this place for 150 years through great famines and wars, but now in time of peace and plenty the community was fading.

Changes in my own life kept pace with changes on the island. When I graduated from secondary school I went to work in the Highlands of Scotland driving tunnels through the mountains. I made high wages at this dangerous work, and some of this money I sent home to my parents, who had retired from the hotel business, and some I sent to Granny in Inishfree. She always wrote back to me and gave me the latest news, which was never good.

Granny's letters portrayed an island that continued to decline and these letters were very depressing to read. I came home to Dungloe once a year and went into the island to visit my grandparents, but this depressed me even more because my grandfather, at ninety seven, had Alzheimer's and did not know me, and my grandmother was very frail. My uncle James did his best to help both of them but it was not easy.

When my grandfather died, I came home for his funeral; and when my grandmother followed him a year later I came home for her funeral as well. With both his parents gone, Uncle James went to live with a niece in Bayonne, New Jersey, and Tim Gallagher's house was abandoned.

Before James turned the key in the front door for the last time, he carefully extinguished the fire in the hearth – a fire that had not been extinguished in that house since 1870, when Tim lit a fire in the new house he had just build for his bride, the former Brigid Doherty, of Dungloe, Co.Donegal. Tim had brought an ember over from his birthplace on Aranmore Island to light the first fire in this new home, and this ember had come from a hearth where the fire had not been extinguished for more than a hundred years either.

This was an ancient custom among the Gaels of northwest Donegal – the custom of never allowing the fire to die. Every night the embers were carefully covered with ashes and every morning the ashes were removed to reveal glowing embers, which would then be coaxed back to life with additions of dry, crisp peat. This went on for generation after generation.

However, James had no one to pass an ember to, so he poured water on the fire, threw the ashes outside, turned the key in the door, and headed off to the United States.

James returned to Donegal once on vacation, but he spent his time on the mainland and never visited the island, because the empty house and the memories of the hard times he suffered during his last few years on the island were too painful and he did not want to open old wounds.

*

The desertion of my grandparent's home foreshadowed what was eventually going to happen to almost every other house on the island. At first it was the younger people who left the island and went to work in Britain, because there was no employment available at home.

This did not create a problem at first, because most of them went away for the summer season, working on British farms, and in the winter they came home and stayed until the following spring or summer. Gradually, however, many of them decided to find year long jobs in Britain and came home only for the Christmas holidays.

With the departure of the young people, the older people felt isolated and alone, especially if they were widows or widowers, and one by one they put out the fires and relocated to the mainland or over to Britain to be near their children.

After the death of my grandparents and the death of my father, I, too, headed abroad as a permanent emigrant. I settled in the United States, where Rose, my sister, and James and Bernie, my brothers, were already settled.

I visited Inishfree for the first time in ten years after coming home on my first vacation from America. I saw dramatic changes. The island culture I had known as a child was in its dead. Not only had more than three quarters of the islanders departed but some of the homes housed people from England and Wales who moved there to live in an environment remote from big city life in Britain.

Some of these people appeared to be devoted to the island and seemed as fond of the atmosphere there as I was when I was a boy and I was at ease in their presence.

But another group had also arrived in the island, who I found difficult to accept. They belonged to a cult made up of English and Irish people who were completely alienated from society and they were using the island as a refuge.

The members of this cult did not really want to associate with anyone. Nicknamed "The Screamers", individuals in this cult used a type of therapy when deeply depressed that annoyed the other residents of the island: they walked off to a remote corner of the island and screamed for hours on end. Supposedly this banished the depression, but it also gave headaches to non-cult members who had to listen to them.

I talked to Margaret Duffy, who was married to Patsy Duffy, during my visit and she tolerated the Screamers although they were hard to put up with. She said they were trying to buy up every house on the island in order to have the whole island to themselves, but most of the owners of houses on the island would not sell to them, even if the house was empty.

Margaret is an author and she loved the isolation of the island, but the activities of the Screamers were making life difficult for her. She was also annoyed at them because she believed they were cruel to the donkeys and goats they owned.

During my visit I walked up towards Tim's house to see what condition the house was in, and on the way up I met two people on the way down the road, both of whom were naked above the waist. One was a woman, whom I found out later was the leader of the cult.

The other person, a young red-headed youth, was half her age and looked slightly disturbed, because he refused to make eye contact, as his eyes wandered all over the place. The woman eyed me curiously and wished me a good afternoon.

I returned the greeting and tried to keep my eyes focused on her face and not on the parts of her naked body between her chin and her belly button. But it was not easy.

I edged past them and continued up the road, resisting the temptation to look back.

When I had climbed the slope to Tim's house I did look back and saw the youth was following me up to the house, while his companion had continued on down the road.

I waited for him to catch up to me and when he did I asked him if he wanted something.

"We want to buy this house," he said. "Are you the owner?"

"This house is not for sale," I said and walked away from him towards the front door of the house, which I found wide open. Inside were a dozen goats lying on a floor filthy with goat manure, and these goats gazed at me insolently, as if I was invading their privacy.

The youth suddenly appeared at the door and the goats got up the minute they saw him.

"Are these your goats?" I asked. "If they are get them out of here and don't let them in here again."

He did not answer me.

I walked up to Aunt Annie's room and found two donkeys having a siesta there. The bed in the room was broken and the donkeys were lying down on the remains of the mattress. The rest of the furniture was missing.

Tim's house had obviously been vandalized: several wardrobes were gone; the dishes on the dresser were missing; and family photographs that had been on the wall were gone.

Of course I did not know whether or not the Screamers were responsible. I knew it was possible that they had simply taken advantage of the situation. But I was angry at them anyway because they had made a byre out of the house.

As the youth looked on, I chased the goats and the donkeys out the door, and then I evicted the youth, whose name I did not get.

As he left I told him if I ever found out that he or any member of his group were trespassing on this house again I would file a complaint with Gardai against them. He said nothing. He just shuffled off avoiding any eye contact.

When he left, I went back down to the beach to Margaret Duffy's house and asked to borrow a hammer and nails. When these were provided to me I went back up to Tim's and nailed shut all the windows and all the doors.

When I was engaged making the house secure I suddenly heard a horrible screaming erupt from somewhere out in the back acres of the property. I immediately thought of my Uncle James and his stories about the banshee living out in a den in that general area. Eventually I got up enough courage to go out the back of the house, and hammer in hand, I scanned the landscape-- but I could see nothing, even though the howling continued.

I gathered up some more courage and walked cautiously towards the area that seemed to be the source of the sound, until I suddenly came upon the red-headed youth, lying behind a mound of dirt howling like a wounded animal. He had all the appearance of someone who was completely demented.

When he saw me he got up and scurried away. I gathered from his screaming that I must have depressed him by turning him out of the house, and he must have decided to give himself some immediate therapy.

As I watched him depart, I thought the island had never in its long history played host to such a bizarre collection of people as these Screamers. I could never have imagined Inishfree being a home to people like that. No wonder the remaining islanders were heading for the mainland in droves.

The Inishfree folk that I had known had a well defined body of rules about social interaction, and they followed these rules religiously.

No Inishfree person would ever trespass on the land of another islander, never mind break into an empty house and stable animals there.

No islander would go around half naked either, or take to howling about their frustrations in another islander's back garden. Law and order had in fact broken down in Inishfree, and anarchy now seemed to reign.

Margaret seemed a little defensive about the Screamers when I talked to her later on about them, saying they were not really that bad when you got to know them. That might have been true, but for me it was dislike at first sight, and I had no intention of getting to know them and would avoid them in future.

Since Margaret said she intended to continue living on the island with her daughter, she organized festivals and other special events in cooperation with Nan Duffy, Patsy's sister, and Maureen and Donal O'Sullivan, who lived in Burtonport but spent a great deal of time promoting the island in the hope of reversing the drain of people from Inishfree. Donal O'Sullivan owned several houses on the island.

The O'Sullivans, Margaret Duffy and others promoting Inishfree persuaded the government to bring electricity to the island, and new piers were built and the roads repaired. They also organized festivals and a writers' group.

Sometimes, during the summer hundreds of people came into the island for island reunions and once again the sound of music, dancing and the laughter of children was everywhere.

I attended one of these festivals with my wife Eileen, my daughter Nora and her husband Trey and we were all delighted with the event. I could see that Nora was beginning to fall under the spell of the island.

However, even though seven of the original 30 houses were renovated as weekend or summer homes, the majority, like Tim's house, stood abandoned, their roofs caving in, the weeds over- running the fields.

Then, one by one, the year-round residents left: the Screamers went to Peru; a Welsh family who were long time residents went out to Dungloe; and an English family, who lived on Inishfree for years, went off to Chicago, and only Margaret Duffy and Barry Pilcher, an English musician, were left to hold the fort.

Finally, Margaret herself took acquired a house in Dungloe and spent most of her time there and only the solitary English immigrant was left as full time resident in this ancient Irish outpost --- chieftain of all he surveyed.

I visited the island in 2005 to take photographs of my grandparents' home while it still stood. I was dropped off at the Scoilt Pier by Oscar Duffy, who runs a ferry service from Burtonport to Inishfree and other islands in the area.

It was a beautiful day just like that summer day long ago when I first came in here with my father, and as I walked over from Scoilt along the beach towards the houses little seemed to have changed at first since my childhood days. Even the larks were serenading me from the heavens.

But then, when the first house on the road, Barney Paddy Bryan's, came into view I saw that it was in ruins, probably battered into submission by the Atlantic gales. This house had been one of the original homes built in Inishfree back in 1735 by A Protestant family from Dungloe named McConnell, who had rented half the island from the landlord. The other half of the island had been rented in 1735 by another Protestant family from Dungloe named Grant, who were relatives of Ulysses S. Grant, the American president. They built the large two-story house that is now owned by the Duffy family and is still in very good condition.

In 1870, my great grandfather, Bryan Gallagher, Tim's father and my mother's grandfather, bought the house from the McConnells, and installed his son Paddy in the farm. He then built another house up on the hill and gave that to Tim., and he split the 40 acres between them.

In the 1890s my father's aunt, Nappy Sweeney from Dungloe, married a man who had bought the Grant house, setting the stage for my father meeting my mother in the island thirty years later.

When I was a child there had been eight houses along the beach, all occupied and all in very good condition. Now two were in ruins, one was on its way out, and one was occupied by Englishman Barry Pilcher, the only full-time resident of the island. The rest were devoted to part time use.

Instead of going up to Tim's to take some photographs, I decided to visit Barry first to see how he was doing. Barry was just fine: he was writing poems, which were being published in Ireland and abroad, and he was composing music, which he played on his saxophone. At one point, he took me out on to the beach and serenaded the larks and the seagulls. The fact that he had the island to himself did not bother him at all.

I wandered over the island for several hours reliving childhood memories and photographing abandoned house and the relatively few that had been repaired as summer residences. It was an eerie experience, like visiting a graveyard in which you were familiar with every name on every tombstone.

Here was a place that had throbbed with life that day back in the summer of 1942 when I first visited Inishfree, a place that was full of vitality and color. It was inconceivable that it had come to this, abandoned like a slum that no one wanted to live in anymore.

I went up to Tim's but took few photographs because the scene was so depressing. The windows and doors were gone and the barns and the henhouse had collapsed. Weeds were running amok everywhere, and my grandfather's gardens had vanished. Inside the house, there was a foot of cow manure on the floor, left there by cattle, which now roamed the island at will, and the plaster was peeling from the walls. The house was not yet dead because the roof was still intact, but death seemed imminent. Here was a house that once throbbed with life: my grandfather and my four uncles played the fiddle, and on winter nights they had entertained their neighbors with the best of Irish fiddle music. Now the music was gone forever.

Apart from wanting photographs of the house before it collapsed I also wanted them to show them to my daughter Nora and her husband Trey Fitzpatrick, who had fallen in love with Inishfree during one of their visits there and were talking about fixing it up. I wanted to show them the extent of the repairs needed. Both of them loved the "splendid isolation" of the island and did not seem to care about the absence of people. Nora was also drawn to the family roots connected with the house.

Trey, who is a hedge fund manager in New York, talked enthusiastically about the possibility of getting a sophisticated computer that would enable him to do his trading from the island. I listened to him with some degree of amazement and wondered how a young man born and raised in Baltimore could be so enchanted by the island.

I then headed down towards Scoilt Pier to wait for Oscar Duffy's ferry that would bring me out Burtonport, where my car was parked on the pier.

As I turned the corner besides the ruins of Barney Paddy Bryan's house I paused and looked at the weed-covered field where Barney had been working the day I arrived on my first visit to the island.

I thought that if Barney and my father were still alive they would be astonished at the fact that Inishfree had been almost completely deserted. I know that I was astounded at the fact that of all the hundreds of people who were on the island when I first visited the place, at this point in time I was the only one of them who was on the island at that particular moment.

EMPTY BEACH

ABANDONED SCHOOL

ABANDONED HOUSE

DONAL O'SULLIVAN AND AUTHOR
OUTSIDE RUINS OF GREAT GRANDFATHER'S HOUSE

INISHFREE   HIGHWAYS

OSCAR DUFFY AND HIS INISHFREE FERRY

As the boat pulled away from the pier and headed out to the bay, I looked at the empty houses that dotted the landscape of Inishfree, all broken-down ghosts of another era, like corpses abandoned to decay in the open.

I saw the big clump of boulders that rose beyond the ruined schoolhouse, the boulders my Uncle James had said was the den of the banshee. I wondered what had happened to the banshee, now that she had nobody but Barry Pilcher to warn about approaching death. Was she still there or had she followed the fleeing islanders to the mainland?

And the black hound – what about him? Had he stayed on the island, or had he also followed the banshee to the mainland? Perhaps, only the fairies remained. Maybe they remained because they did not need people and they might be delighted with the privacy and glad to have the island to themselves.

As Inishfree drifted off into the distance I was not without hope that the island might spring back to life again, perhaps as a popular weekend hideaway.

Perhaps my two grandchildren, Joseph and Nellie, would discover the magic of the place and spend some time there with friends while they were young enough to enjoy it.

But I knew that my own affection for the island was not just based on beautiful landscapes alone – it was also based on my deep relationship with scores of people, and it was this combination of family ties and memorable scenery that had won my heart from the very first day.

The family members were all gone now, and even though the island was as beautiful as ever it no longer held me spellbound: it was a ghost of its former self, and it had become just another attractive place to visit.

*

BARNEY RUA'S BAR

Barney Rua's Bar was not the most popular watering hole in Greystones, Co. Donegal, nor was it the most successful from a financial point of view. But Barney was able to attract enough steady customers to insure that he made a very nice living, and, over the years, he had accumulated a very healthy bank account-- an account that insured that he would have a comfortable retirement.

Barney selected those he wanted as steady customers very carefully. He was very attentive to those customers whom he valued as a definite asset, and he was not that friendly to any customer who wandered in who did not fit the profile of an ideal customer, and before long these customers drifted off to other bars in Greystones that offered them a warmer welcome.

Barney's ideal customers fell into three main categories. First, there were the talented storytellers who were Barney Rua's greatest asset, because it was they who made the bar such an interesting place to visit. There were about six of these men among Barney's patrons, and although there were evenings when none of them were around to spin their yarns, there were at least one of them there at various times during the week, and over the years they helped build up the perception that Barney's Bar was a place that had among its patrons the best storytellers in the town..

The second group was comprised of those that Barney classified as "good listeners." These were very important to the mix of clients, because they provided an attentive audience for the storytellers. Without this audience, the storytellers would not be inspired to spin a yarn at all and the bar's reputation would suffer as a result.

The third category, and there was only a few in this group, were the ones who would sometimes challenge an aspect of a story, thereby provoking a debate with the storyteller, and sometimes getting the storyteller to react with annoyance. These customers added spice to the evening's entertainment.

Barney's role was to stage manage all the discussions and to act as referee if a discussion seemed to be getting out of hand. He never told a story himself and never took part in the discussions, but he projected an image of being deeply interested in everything that was talking place on the other side of the counter.

There was one other trait that was very important if one was to be accepted as a valued customer by Barney. This was the ability to buy and consume a half a dozen pints of Guinness or two or three glasses of whiskey during an evening at the bar and do so without staggering around or picking fights with other patrons. Barney would not tolerate anyone who could not hold their drink, or who thought they could sit in Barney's establishment all night and buy only one pint of Guinness.

Over the years, Barney had built up a core group of about one hundred customers who did all their drinking in the bar. On any given day there was between ten and fifteen of them patronizing the establishment, consuming considerable amounts of alcohol and amusing each other by discussing world politics or by telling tall tales based on a wide variety of subjects. These patrons were the bedrock on which Barney's little empire was built.

Barney opened his bar Monday through Saturday, from 4 P.M. to Midnight -- he never did business on Sunday, and every Sunday he cleaned the bar from top to bottom early in the day, and then went off to play golf in the afternoon.

Barney had very good business reasons for not opening his bar until late in the afternoon and keeping it closed completely on Sundays.

When he first inherited the bar he continued with the practice established by his father and grandfather, who had owned the bar before him, of opening the bar at 10 A.M. every day, including Sunday.

But after the first three years he became aware that many of his early morning customers were alcoholics who came into his bar every morning with shaking hands and frazzled nerves looking for a cure, and some of these were frequently looking for credit because they had spent all their money the night before.

Barney disliked this type of customer intensely and he had a number of reasons for this dislike. First of all, he was a teetotaler himself and had little tolerance for anyone who had lost the battle with alcohol addiction. He viewed alcohol as a social lubricant and not a ball and chain, and he believed that anyone who could not handle it should give it up, just as he had when his drinking got out of hand many years previously. He also disliked alcoholics for business reasons: alcoholics made social drinkers uncomfortable and for this reason he thought that catering to alcoholics was bad for business.

His father and grandfather had put up with this kind of customer and over the years wound up being owed money, which was never paid.

Barney decided that he was going to try to attract a different type of clientele, a more upscale type of clientele, and a clientele that would establish Barney Rua's Bar as a place where the conversation was first class and everyone knew how to hold their Guinness.

So, he abandoned the morning trade entirely by not opening until 4 PM, thereby forcing his alcoholic clients to patronize some other establishment.

He refused to open on Sundays for several reasons. First of all, he thought that six days were enough for any man to work, and working a seventh day only made him a slave to the bar, which he found unacceptable. So, by closing on Sundays and only opening for eight hours during the week, he was only working a 48-hour week, instead of the 100-hour week worked by some other bar owners.

Another reason for closing on Sundays was the clientele that poured into the bars in Greystones after the Sunday Mass, which was usually made up of men who drank only once a week and got drunk easily. These men drank one drink after another as quickly as possible in order to get as much drink on board before their wives or girlfriends came looking for them. When their woman folk finally caught up with them they were usually drunk and a loud noisy argument sometimes followed, and Barney was often dragged into these quarrels because he was blamed for getting the men drunk in the first place.

After several years of this Barney decided that he did not want this type of clientele anymore, and the only way to get rid of them was not to open at all on Sundays. So, every Sunday morning Barney cleaned the bar from top to bottom and made sure the place was spotless before he went off to play golf. The only departure from this Sunday routine was on the first Sunday of each month when a middle-aged unmarried woman arrived at Barney's apartment above the bar, supposedly to help him clean his living quarters, but in reality her duties also included a little romance with Barney, which earned her an additional bonus. They had been involved in this routine for years.

Barney was a reasonably handsome man and was perceived to be wealthy and he could have had his pick of the single woman in Greystones, but he absolutely refused to date any of them or get involved in any romantic entanglements. The idea of marriage gave him nightmares.

Barney's horror of marriage was based on his experience of living with his parents and grandparents who fought like cats and dogs while they were alive and even got involved in physical violence when all four of them got drunk at the same time, which happened frequently.

Barney had got involved in the fighting and drinking when he was a teenager, but when he inherited the bar, he quit drinking entirely and swore off romance as well. He did make one concession to pleasure, however, and that was his monthly romp with the cleaning lady.

Barney was a creature of habit. He got up every morning at 7 A.M. and immediately went into the shower. After his shower he shaved carefully and then put on clean underwear and a different suit, shirt and tie that he had worn the previous day. He was obsessive about his image and was contemptuous of some of his customers who wore the same clothes day in and day out and who rarely, if ever, took a shower.

He tidied up the bathroom and made his bed before he headed for the kitchen for daily breakfast of wheat flakes, toast, soft boiled eggs, and tea. It would never occur to him to vary his diet in any way, because he enjoyed this particular breakfast so much.

After breakfast Barney mopped the kitchen floor, washed the dishes, and tidied up to make sure everything was in its own place.

By 8 A.M., he left Greystones for his daily hour-long walk in the countryside, and by 9 A.M., he was back in his apartment above the bar with two Irish and one English daily newspaper he picked up every morning in Reilly's shop. The rest of the morning and early afternoon, with a brief time out for lunch, was spent reading the newspapers, and absorbing the information in the magazines he subscribed to – *Time, Newsweek,* and *National Geographic,* three American publications that he believed provided him with a well-rounded education on world affairs.

Barney never revealed his knowledge of world affairs to anyone except the local Protestant Minister, who sometimes visited Barney in his private apartment on a Sunday afternoon. The pair of them would then engage in long discussions on a wide variety of subjects, both very pompous, each trying to out do the other with intellectual riffs.

Barney served the rector port wine and biscuits during these intellectual skirmishes, and the rector stayed with Barney until he felt the alcohol impairing his ability to argue, and then he ambled off into the evening.

Barney never explained to anyone what the rector was doing in his apartment, and people being what they are attributed the worst motivation to these visits, namely that the two of them were romantically involved. But, this of course was not true, because Barney was involved with the housekeeper.

Barney's attraction to the rector was based on his belief that the rector was the only person in the parish that he could have an intelligent discussion with. However, Barney believed that he himself was the most educated person in Greystones and that intellectually he was far superior to anyone else in the town, including the rector.

There were times when Barney could barely conceal his contempt for his customers when a debate erupted and he was convinced that both sides to the debate knew very little about the subject they were debating.

There were two subjects which Barney disliked to hear discussed in his establishment: one was religion, which he believed should not be debated at all; the other was supernatural events like ghosts, poltergeists or phenomena of this nature, which Barney did not believe in. He eventually succeeded in making the subject of religion off-limits on the grounds that his three Protestant customers were deeply offended by the opinion sometimes expressed by a few Catholic customers -- that all Protestants are heretics.

But since ghost stories were the most popular of all stories told in the bar, he had to allow these to be told in order to keep his customers happy.

However, Barney's intellectual arrogance made him contemptuous of those who believed in any type of supernatural occurrence, and this included, in his opinion, any belief in organized religion, which he categorized as just another form of superstition that had no basis in reality.

Of course Barney was too astute a businessman to express his opinions in public, and he was even a big enough hypocrite to attend Mass every Sunday, which he justified to himself on the grounds that no Christian living in Greystones would patronize a bar that they knew was owned by an atheist, because they believed God would strike them dead if they did.

So, for business reasons he made his way up to the Church every Sunday morning, and for businesses reasons he tried not to look disgusted at the pointless sermons made every week on the altar.

Barney contributed as the basket was passed around, and gave enough not to look too cheap, but not too much to look too generous. Barney knew how to strike a balance.

The ghost stories sometimes told in the bar were a different matter. He endured the ghost stories, again for strictly business reasons, but he secretly despised all of those who were absolutely convinced of the existence of such beings.

In private, he was grateful that his own mind had long ago been cleansed of all base superstitions and religious beliefs. If he was ever forced to reveal how he really saw himself he would describe himself as a scholar, a scientist, and an atheist.

Barney's self image remained firmly in place for thirty years, until the night Oscar McCann walked in the door with Bonzo, his pet bulldog in tow. By the end of the night, Barney's self image was shattered, and he would never again be convinced that science had an answer for all questions, and that only the truly ignorant believed in supernatural phenomena.

When Oscar and Bonzo entered the bar, Barney felt that flutter of nervousness he always felt when the bulldog was around, because the dog had a habit of staring at Barney with liquid black eyes that oozed venom. The dog could stare at Barney for hours on end, never once turning to look at anyone else.

Barney was convinced the dog hated him, and years back he had insisted that McCann have a leash on the dog when he brought him to the bar, and that the leash was tied to the handle of the closet door, so that Bonzo could not lunge at anyone. He also insisted that McCann stand near the dog in order to keep an eye on him.

BONZO

BARNEY RUA'S BAR

Barney's nervousness about the dog had a firm base in reality, and everyone in the bar knew this, because over the years, the dog had lunged at a number of people, and twice he had inflicted bites. Only Oscar's cozy relationship with the Gardai saved Bonzo from the firing squad, but his reprieve was given on the understanding that the dog was never allowed to roam the streets, and was only allowed out if he was on a leash and Oscar was with him

But even though Bonzo was firmly tied up, Barney was still not at ease because the dog stared at him for hours on end with evident hostility and Barney believed the dog would like nothing better than to tear him to shreds, for reasons known only to the dog himself.

Barney had never met a dog like this and he knew hundreds of dogs over the years. The dogs Barney had come across in his life came in all shapes and sizes and with all kinds of dispositions: some were mean; some aloof; some very friendly. All seemed to have limited intelligence, and a few seemed to have a distinct personality.

Bonzo did not fit the mold of any dog of Barney's acquaintance: he was smart, macho and was obviously his own person. Bonzo was also evidently convinced that Barney was the dregs of humanity and Barney could never understand what the dog had against him.

If Oscar were not one of Barney's best customers who was also a close friend of a number of the other customers, Barney would have insisted that Oscar leave Bonzo at home. And if Oscar refused, he would have banned both of them from the establishment. But Barney knew Bonzo was Oscar's best friend and he was afraid of the consequences if he threw him out. So he viewed the dog as a penance he had to put up with.

Oscar was in the pub for about an hour, consuming Guinness and John Jameson in reasonable quantities, when Eamon Sweeney, who had a long-standing grievance against Oscar, looked over at Oscar and said: " I hear that your uncle's house is haunted. I hear it is not safe to go anywhere near it at night ... or in the daytime for that matter."

Sweeney knew that Oscar did not believe in ghosts, because he ridiculed those who said they believed in them, and he also knew it would infuriate Oscar to claim that his uncle's house, which had been vacant since the uncle died more than a year previously, was being haunted by his uncle, or some other supernatural being. Oscar would take such talk as a provocative insult because it implied that his uncle, who had been a deeply religious man, had failed to go to heaven and was instead rambling around the old house.

Oscar did not respond to Sweeney, because he knew that Sweeney was trying to provoke him, and he had no intention of giving satisfaction to the man, so he ignored Sweeney's statement.

Barney was watching as the little drama unfolded and was glad that someone had decided to add a little spice to the social interaction, since so far that evening there had been no excitement at all in the pub.

But he was a little uneasy at this particular exchange, because there was such bad blood between these two. Still a little excitement was better than no excitement at all.

However, had Barney known what the outcome of this little drama would be, he would have evicted Sweeney from the bar immediately because Sweeney was inadvertently setting in motion a series of events that would shatter Barney's carefully constructed way of life.... permanently.

Hugh Doherty saw that Oscar was not going to take the bait, so he decided to keep the ball rolling by responding to Sweeney's statement about the haunted house himself.

"Did you hear what exactly is going on in the house? Did anyone see anything, or hear anything?" said Doherty.

"There are all kinds of stories making the rounds, "said Sweeney. "Lights going on and off during the night. Sounds like banshees crying. And a man dressed in a black robe walking up the lane from the house. You wouldn't get me to go anywhere near the place – not for all the tea in China."

Other customers added to tale by relating stories they had heard, and gradually Oscar got so annoyed that he finally had to respond.

"I think all of you are a bunch of old women who have nothing better to do than defame the memory of a man whose shoes you were not fit to polish. There are no ghosts in that house. I was there earlier today and I saw or heard nothing. I'll tell you what I will do. I will take Sweeney here, or anyone else for that matter, down to the house right now to see if there are any ghosts down there. I will even take Bonzo here with us, and Bonzo will protect you, because that dog is not afraid of man, beast, or ghost of any description. I don't think he would even be afraid of the devil himself."

Dead silence greeted Oscar's challenge at first. Then Sweeney said he wouldn't go because he did not want to leave his wife a widow. And he told Oscar he should not put himself in harm's way either because he had a wife, too, who depended on him for support.

Several other patrons in the bar echoed Sweeney's sentiments, and the more they urged Oscar not to do anything foolish the more infuriated he became.

But when Barney intervened and told everyone to leave Oscar alone, this was the last straw as far as Oscar was concerned, because he believed that Barney was patronizing him.

"Alright, me and Bonzo will go down there alone," he said. "And to prove to you that I was in the house I will take back that big statue of the Blessed Virgin that is in the front window. I have the keys to the house right here in my pocket."

Oscar then untied Bonzo's leash and the pair of them headed out the door. All the patrons heard him open the door of his car, and a moment later they heard him drive off in the direction of Joe's house, a mile away.

Barney was the first to speak after Oscar and Bonzo left the pub.

"God forgive you for teasing him like that," he said. "You all know right well he has been very upset about his Uncle Joe's death; you all know Joe was like a father to him after his father died. Why would you be so hard on him by pretending the house is haunted?"

"I don't know about any of the rest of them but I wasn't pretending at all," said Hugh Doherty. "My brother Mickey told me that he got a fright when he was passing the house the other night: he said he saw old Joe looking out the kitchen window."

"Well, I might have been teasing him a little," said Sweeney, "But I can tell you there is a lot of people in the parish who are convinced that the old man is not resting easily in his grave."

Barney looked at Sweeney for a moment and was tempted to say what was on his mind: that he knew the real reason Sweeney wanted to annoy Oscar, but he held his tongue.

Oscar had given Sweeney a bad beating fifteen years previously, when they got into a fight over a girl both had been dating. Oscar won the fight and the girl, who later became his wife. But he had made an enemy of Sweeney for life.

The patrons drifted into an uneasy silence as they waited for Oscar to return.

When ten minutes passed without any sign of Oscar or Bonzo, Barney opened the front door and looked out into the night. Uncle Joe's house was located at the far end of the village from the pub, set back from the main road by several hundred yards. A long lane connected the house to the road, and a score of pine trees surrounded the house insuring its privacy.

When he did not see or hear anything, Barney closed the door gently and went back behind the bar. Silence continued to rule the establishment.

Hugh Doherty was the first to hear the sound, a faint howling, and when he opened the front door to see where it was coming from, the howling seemed to increase, and gradually it took on the tone of a tortured soul that had escaped from Hell.

Doherty backed away from the open door, his face ashen. "The dog's coming and he seems insane," he said. "What the hell could be wrong with him?"

Barney started to come out from behind the counter to close the door, but he had only taken a few steps across the floor, when the dog came careening through the door, eyes wild, and froth coming from his mouth, and he bolted under a table at the far end of the bar and collapsed in a quivering heap. Barney immediately retreated behind the counter.

"Would someone tie up that dog", he said, but no one moved.

All of those present looked at the open door with apprehension afraid of the appearance of whatever it was that had reduced Bonzo to a helpless wreck. There was no sign of Oscar.

For the first time in his adult life, Barney experienced fear of the unknown, and his voice had a quiver when he told Daugherty to close the door.

But Doherty had no intention of going near the door and he curtly told Barney to close the door himself. But Barney stayed where he was, afraid not only of the unknown, but also of the dog, who was still not tied up.

More than five minutes passed in dead silence, a silence broken only by the moaning and panting of the dog. Barney and all the other patrons were waiting for the return of Oscar's car.

Then, Oscar suddenly appeared in the door, hyperventilating and completely disheveled, his clothes filthy and his hands and face covered with scrapes and cuts. He looked like he had been attacked by a wild animal.

"What happened to you," said Barney, horrified at Oscar's appearance. "What happened to you and the dog?"

Oscar staggered over to the bar and tried to speak, but the words failed to emerge. He seemed struck dumb.

Barney quickly poured him a glass of Jameson and a pint of Guinness and Oscar attacked both greedily.

But it took a second glass of whiskey and another Guinness before he regained the power of speech and was able to communicate in short sentences what had happened to him.

When he had finished his story, Barney looked at him with a combination of contempt and disgust, as if Oscar's explanation ridiculous.

"You mean to tell me that you didn't see or hear a thing up at that house, and that this whole hullabaloo is about the dog suffering a panic attack and running away, and you running after him terrified because the animal was terrified? How did your face get cut and your clothes filthy?"

"I fell several times on the way here. I tripped and fell. You don't know what it was like, Barney. The minute I pulled into the front of the house and the headlights lit up the house the dog went wild in the car. He kept staring at the house and howling. He went off his head.

"He was trying to crash through the windshield and crash through the side windows, and he went to hell completely when the engine suddenly died and the headlights went out. I couldn't get the car started again, so I opened the door and he ran up the lane like the devil himself was after him. I tried to leave the car and go after him, but something banged the door in my face. But I got out the other side anyway and ran up the lane and I was sure something was after me, although I did not see anything. I thought I would go off my head. Bonzo is the toughest dog in the world and I knew that if he was scared I should be twice as scared."

As Oscar spoke, he kept looking over at Bonzo, who still lay in a quivering heap under the table. Oscar went over to him and tried to pet him, but the dog bared his teeth and Oscar backed off. Sweeney, who was not one to miss an opportunity, said that the dog must be blaming Oscar for what had happened, but Oscar did not respond to him.

It was obvious that Barney could not make a great deal of sense out of Oscar's story, and once again he cross-examined Oscar about the story.

"You did not see or hear anything?" he said.

"No, I didn't," Oscar said. "But when I was running up that lane I had this terrible feeling that there was something following me that didn't want me there. I was never as frightened in all my life."

Everyone in the bar, except Barney, had little trouble accepting what seemed to be an obvious fact: Oscar and his dog had a run in with the supernatural. They also accepted that the dog was more sensitive to the presence of the supernatural than Oscar, because he had raised the red alert first. To the patrons this was a prime example of the existence of another world that was inhabited by all kinds of supernatural beings, and they accepted it as part of the reality they lived in.

But Barney had spent a lifetime dismissing ghost stories and despising those who believed in them and now he was confused about what had taken place. Barney could write off Oscar's terror to an overripe imagination, but the bulldog was another matter entirely. This dog was now frightening him in a whole new way.

An unnatural silence descended on the bar because most of the patrons did not know what to say to Oscar or how to react to his obvious distress. So they all remained very quiet for some time, but then one by one they started to leave the pub, giving various reasons why they were leaving.

But the real reason was that they were embarrassed by the situation and they wanted to get out of it with as much grace as possible. The inhabitants of Greystones have no talent for hiding embarrassment and their instinct is to run away from any situation that causes it.

When there was only a few patrons left, the bulldog also decided to call it a night and headed with a staggering gait towards the door.

Oscar got off his stool and opened the door for the dog, who then stared out into the black night for a few minutes, carefully looking to the right and then to the left as if he were searching for something.

Oscar stood behind him motionless, and Barney and the remaining patrons watched the pair silently.

Suddenly the dog left the doorway and sped down the street towards Oscar's home, with Oscar galloping along behind him.

The departure of the pair was a signal for all but one of the customers to drink up and head out the door without a word, leaving only Barney and Eamon Sweeney left of the twenty who had been there when the incident began.

Barney was very upset at this turn of events and he felt compelled to blame someone.

"This is all your fault he said to Sweeney. If you hadn't opened your big mouth none of this would have happened."

Sweeney was astonished at this sudden attack, because this was the first time that Barney had ever said a cross word to him. But he felt compelled to defend himself.

"I didn't turn the ghosts loose on him; I had nothing to do with that."

"There are no ghosts," said Barney, "There are just superstitious minds, and you are very good at provoking them."

Sweeney did not argue with him, because he was very nervous about the entire incident, and not the least of his nervousness came from the knowledge that he had to pass Old Joe's house before he came to his own home, and he would not be human if he were not apprehensive about what he might meet on the road. But after twenty minutes of fiddling with his glass of Guinness he left the Guinness and walked out the door without a word, leaving Barney alone.

As he stood behind the bar, Barney was aware he was suffering from shock over what had happened, and he also could feel panic surging through his emotions. Not since he was a small boy had he reacted with terror to ghost stories, and now this incident had transported him back to his childhood.

Barney was embarrassed and frightened by his fear. He had thought that he had put such panic behind him long ago when he abandoned religious and superstitious beliefs in favor of the truths of science, but here was the panic back again, stronger than ever.

Barney decided to close the bar early and go up to his apartment and try to sort out the conflicting emotions that swirled around in his mind.

He had never before closed the bar down at 8 P.M., but he had no customers and even if he had he was in no mood to be the good host.

As he entered the large spacious apartment above the bar, which had been home to his parents and grandparents before him, he experienced a host of unwanted memories that made him even more nervous than he had been before. As he walked into the living room he had flashbacks to the wakes held for each of his parents and for each of his father's parents.

Looking into the dining room, he saw the table that had been used to hold the coffins. And all around the walls were portraits of parents, grandparents, uncles, aunts, great uncles and great aunts, and even a portrait of his great grandparents, all of whom were dead for many years, and now they seemed to stare down at him from the walls with expressions that Barney interpreted as hostile. Not one of them was smiling.

The level of anxiety that he was experiencing escalated.

But the portraits of the ancient dead did not disturb him half as much as his inability to get the dog out of his mind – the dog that had been transformed from the terrorist of the village into a quivering coward in less than an hour. He could not conceive of a single scientific explanation for the dog's transformation, and his mind kept returning to the same frightening conclusion: Bonzo had been exposed to the supernatural and it had terrified him.

The idea that there were supernatural entities out there and that he too might be exposed to them drove Barney to the edge of a panic attack, and to ward it off he took a bottle of Jameson out of a cabinet and poured himself a large glass of Ireland's strongest whiskey. Barney had given up drinking forty years previously because he knew he was developing a need for it, and he did not want to go down the road his grandfather and his father had gone because of alcohol – to an early grave.

But his fear of the unknown this night was greater than his fear of alcohol, and he gulped down the whiskey and then had another glass.

Sometime during the night, in the small hours of the morning, Barney staggered out of his apartment and strode up the deserted streets of Greystones towards the graveyard. When he arrived at graveyard he stopped at the grave of each relative and unleashed a torrent of abuse which consisted of all the grievances he had against them when they were alive. When he unburdened himself of all this venom he went back to his apartment.

Barney woke up on the living room floor the following morning, an empty whiskey bottle beside him, and with no memory of how he consumed the entire bottle, although he had a vague memory of the graveyard.

However, he had a very clear memory of what had happened before he started to drink: he remembered the panic-stricken dog, and his own terror which had washed over him in waves.

He did not leave the house that day at all, but instead spent the morning in bed nursing a hangover, and spent the afternoon taking family portraits off the wall and storing them in a closet. He did this because he felt his dead relatives were still staring at him.

He opened the bar on time, and very quickly the bar was full of customers, some of whom had not been there the previous night but who wanted to know all about what had happened to Oscar and Bonzo. Barney decided to plead ignorance of what had happened, and his only comment on the incident was that Oscar said the dog had a panic attack up at the abandoned home. Barney pretended that this was a minor event and he could not see what the fuss was all about.

But when word arrived at the bar that the dog had died and that Oscar was taken to the hospital suffering from "nerves," the story became a sensation and the event was distorted and exaggerated to the extent that some people were claiming that the Devil had appeared to Oscar and his dog, and this was what had driven them out of their minds.

Barney did his best to endure all the excitement in the days and weeks that followed, but the stress took its toll.

First, he was unable to get through the day without imbibing whiskey periodically, and then he found he had great difficulty sleeping, because if he drifted off at all he immediately was plunged into a maelstrom of nightmares, featuring Bonzo and many of his dead relatives. The only relief he got was when he consumed more whiskey.

Barney's slide into alcoholism was slow and painful, but his problems were not noticed by his customers at first.

A change in his behavior was first noticed when he began to have a drink with his customers, and later on he became quarrelsome, which was very unusual for him. Finally he prohibited all talk about ghosts in his bar, especially any talk about the dead Bonzo, or about Oscar who had eventually had to be incarcerated in a mental institution. None of his customers linked his behavior to the night the dog lost his mind, because Barney never came right out to say that the dog was the source of his problems.

But the truth was that Barney was adrift, because the dog's behavior destroyed his conviction that the supernatural did not exist, and once he entertained the idea that the supernatural did exist he was not able to cope with it.

Slowly he drifted down the road to self destruction taken by his father and his grandfather.

One year later, by the time Barney had committed suicide by hanging himself in the bar, Barney's customers had long departed, frightened away by his periodic delusions that his father and grandfather were visiting him during the night, and by his claims that Bonzo was howling in his backyard.

Nobody liked ghost stories more than Barney's patrons did; indeed, it was their love of ghost stories that had attracted them to Barney's Bar in the first place.

But their love of ghost stories was based on their entertainment value, while Barney's tales generated terror in his listeners, partly because the tales were so creepy, but mainly because the storyteller was gradually turning into a madman, and Barney's customers feared madmen much more than they feared ghosts.

One by one his patrons drifted away, and in the end he presided over an empty bar, talking to himself and consuming bottle after bottle of whiskey.

Barney's Bar closed down after he had killed himself, and before long stories started to circulate that the building was haunted. Some people said they saw lights go on and off in the apartment above the bar; others said they heard a dog howling in the empty bar late at night or early in the morning just before dawn, which was the time that Barney took his own life.

Melly's Pub became the new meeting place for Barney's patrons, and the tradition of telling ghost stories was resumed there. One night Tom Melly, the owner, said that he would give a year's supply of whiskey to any man who would spend a night alone in Barney Rua's Bar. He said he would get the keys from Barney's cousin.

Dead silence greeted this offer.

There were no takers.

End

GHOSTS?

I was a firm believer in the supernatural until I was in my early twenties. I accepted without question the teachings of the Catholic Church, and I believed in the existence of ghosts and a whole array of supernatural beings.

Then I went through a period of several decades in which I questioned all my beliefs in Heaven, Hell or in the existence of ghosts, poltergeists or any other supernatural being. During this period I did not become an atheist, but I certainly was not very far removed from an atheist's attitude to all aspects of organized religion.

Eventually, however, I had a number of personal experiences which was hard to reconcile with the belief system of an atheist. These experiences did not make me revert to the unquestioning believer I had been in my youth, but they left the door open to the idea that some sort of life beyond the grave is possible.

I was raised in a mainly Roman Catholic community in northwest Donegal that was intolerant of atheism. I did not know anyone who claimed to be an atheist, and very few that expressed any doubts about Jesus being a Catholic. I believed that that the fires of Hell awaited all those who died in a state of sin; that priests had powers beyond the understanding of ordinary people; that Protestants would suffer eternal damnation; and that the Catholic Church had the last word on all matters concerning life and death..

In addition to those basic beliefs subscribed to by me and the majority of other residents of the area, there was a belief in a whole body of pagan folklore that incorporated a belief in holy wells, haunted house, banshees, omens, and a whole array of ghosts and poltergeists into their Catholic faith.

Many of these additional beliefs had their roots in pagan Ireland, but they were not seen as being openly in conflict with the teachings of the Catholic Church because the priests were inclined to tolerate these pagan superstitions. The priests preferred to let sleeping dogs lie.

For instance, there were holy wells in the area that had been popular long before the arrival of Christianity, and I have not known any priest who condemned these wells as the last outposts of Pagan Ireland, or told people they should not believe in miraculous cures that had occurred   there.

During my formative years I never thought of God as a supreme being who loved me, or of Heaven as a place I looked forward to living in. My reaction to anything supernatural was an overwhelming sense of fear. This fear was generated by sermons at Mass that focused on the horrifying punishment that was waiting for those who did not adhere to the doctrines of the Church, including images of lost souls tumbling into the infernos of hell, and these images terrified me.

When I was a boy, there was an order of monks who conducted a preaching mission in the parish periodically, and these monks were expert at putting the fear of God into all those who listened to their fire and brimstone diatribes every night that the mission lasted.

I went away from those sermons afraid that if I died suddenly during the night while in a state of sin I would plunge down to the pits of hell. I was terrified after the mission ended, and it took me many weeks to recover from this terror, but eventually I made a recovery and then I went back to my usual sinful behavior. Time is the great ally of the sinner.

But the fear generated by the clergy had numerous by-products.

One was an extreme nervousness about being anywhere near graveyards at night, especially Protestant graveyards. Another was a conviction that ghosts walked the land after dark.

The existence of ghosts was of course a product of a conviction that there was a hereafter, and in this hereafter there were some people who did not die in a state of God's grace and were doomed to return to earth and wander around as lost souls.

I believed in the hereafter and I believed in ghosts, and I was always very much afraid of running into one when I was out at night.

My acceptance of everything I was taught in Church survived into my teenage years. Then, when I was eighteen I read a book about the history of the papacy, and in this book it was revealed that many of the popes in centuries gone by were bigger sinners than I was, and had committed all kinds of crimes, including murder. This revelation undermined many of my basic spiritual beliefs and led me to question a great deal of what I had been taught as a youth.

A fear of the priests and bishops was the first casualty of my new attitude. I then edged towards a theory that all this talk of Heaven and Hell, ghosts and poltergeists, was nothing more than the superstitions generated by fear of the unknown.

As the years passed, however, I would have three experiences that I found very difficult to explain if I was to rule out any supernatural explanation.

The first of these events occurred when I returned from America for a vacation in northwest Donegal.

During my stay in Donegal I went to visit Jim Doherty, a friend of mine who had a summer house in South Donegal and who invited me to stay overnight with him.

Jim and I had worked together for several years in New Jersey, and both of us visited Donegal at least once a year.

Jim's summer house was out in a rural area on a small farm and there was only one other house close by, which was occupied by a middle aged farmer named McLeod, who lived there with his wife.

Jim introduced me to McLeod and his wife shortly after I arrived, and I came to the conclusion that the farmer was a bit of an oddball, because he seemed very tense and never looked at you directly, even when you were talking to him. His wife, on the other hand, was a friendly gregarious woman who talked to you like she had known you all her life.

Jim's sitting room overlooked McLeod's back yard and in the course of the evening I saw McLeod coming in and out of his house and going into a barn that was at the back of the yard. He was always accompanied by a beautiful collie dog that trotted behind him everywhere he went.

I was not deliberately watching McLeod's movements because the armchair I was sitting in gave me a view of the McLeod yard, so I could see his activities even as I talked to Jim.

Just as it was getting dark, McLeod walked out the back door of his house again and strode directly across the yard to the barn, with his faithful collie trotting along behind.

McLeod had a gray metal bucket in his hand and I presumed he had some food in it for the young calf I saw him bring into the barn an hour before.

About ten minutes after McLeod entered the barn he emerged again, bucket in hand and the faithful collie trotting after him. I remembered smiling at the spectacle at first because the pair seemed like such bosom buddies.

I noticed immediately, however, that McLeod seemed to have a peculiar gait: he seemed very light on his feet, unlike the flat-footed stride I had seen him use all afternoon. He did not turn towards the back door of his house, as he had done all afternoon, but walked straight ahead towards the front gate, which led out towards the main road.

As he passed directly across the yard in front of me he turned his head and stared at me directly in through the window with a very peculiar expression on his face, as if he were deeply saddened by something. The dog also turned and looked at me briefly, and then turned away. After that both went out the front gate and disappeared from my view.

I was about to say something to Jim about how peculiar McLeod had looked, but I decided not to because I didn't know how to describe it. I knew the look McLeod had given me was odd, and it was the first time he had looked directly at me, but I didn't know how to describe it to Jim, so I said nothing and continued the conversation.

Fifteen minutes later Mrs. McLeod came out of the house and looked around the yard. Then she began to call out her husband's name.

Jim heard her and looked out the window. He stared at the woman for a minute. "She keeps a tight rein on the old man," he said. "She doesn't let him out of her sight. He used to pretend to go out to work in the fields, but instead he would sneak off to McGovern's Bar down the road and get fluttered. Then he would come back to the house and throw his weight around. She hated his drinking and more than once she went down to McGovern's Bar and pulled him out of there. Now she checks on him every fifteen minutes."

I was about to tell him that McLeod had taken off out the front gate and was probably down in McGovern's as we spoke, but I decided to mind my own business because I did not want to get involved in a family fight.

Mrs. McLeod continued to call her husband, and when she got no response she strode deliberately across the yard towards the barn, anger displayed in very step she took. But she was in the barn less than a minute when she came running out shrieking at the top of her voice: "Help me God, help me god!"

Jim and I both ran out to find out what was wrong. When we got to her, she was sobbing: "He hung himself in the barn," she said. I could not believe what she was saying because I had just seen him go out the gate – him and the dog. And I still didn't believe her until I went into the barn and saw him slowly swinging at the end of a rope, with the collie lying beneath him, quivering and whimpering.

I found the scene utterly unbelievable, not only because of the suicide, but because of the apparition that had moved across the yard moments before, and the shock must have been written all over my face.

Jim thought that my physical reaction in the barn was the result of seeing the body and he quickly escorted me out of the barn and into his house, where he handed me a glass of whiskey. He then called the Gardai and told them about McLeod's death. He told me to lie on the couch and relax while he went out to console Mrs. McLeod and await the arrival of the Gardai.

I did not tell Jim about the apparition I saw in the yard. I said nothing about it to the Gardai either, or to Mrs. McLeod, or to anyone else, and I only told Jim when we were back in America.

When I did eventually tell him he acted at first like I was playing a prank on him, and then he tried to pass off my story as something that was the result of the stress I had experienced when I saw the body. When I told him I saw the apparition *before* I saw the body, he said my memory was playing tricks on me.

"You only think you saw it before you saw the body, but you really couldn't have. You know perfectly well that that is impossible."

I knew where he was coming from with that statement.

We had many discussions about religion and Irish superstitions and I knew he was an atheist who did not believe in the supernatural at all.

So I dropped the matter and never brought it up again, although from time to time he would tease me about the McLeod ghost.

But this was an incident that prevented me from becoming an atheist like Jim. Although I might dismiss the vast majority of ghost stories told to me, in the back of my mind I was always aware of seeing McLeod's ghost stroll across the yard while his body swung from a rafter in the barn, and I have no way of explaining this without turning to the supernatural for an explanation.

No way at all.

*

The second of these incidents occurred in Monkstown, County Dublin, and again it occurred when I was home from the United States on vacation and was visiting my sister Annie, who lived in Monkstown.

However, this time it did not involve an apparition: I did not see or hear anything; but it was a frightening experience nevertheless, and it confirmed the opinion that I arrived at after the Donegal incident -- that some events defy logic or science and only make sense if viewed as examples of the supernatural.

My sister Annie and her husband lived in a big rambling Victorian townhouse. Annie was a teacher and her husband Jerome was a banker, and both worked in Monkstown. My brother Bernie was also home from America at the same time, and he also stayed with Annie the night I was there.

Jerome went back to work at the bank after dinner, and Annie, Bernie and I were left alone for the rest of the evening exchanging stories about growing up in Dungloe, County Donegal, and updating each other about how our lives were going up to this point.

The conversation all evening was about family matters and at no time did the conversation turn to the subject of ghosts, because ghosts were rarely if ever talked about in Campbell family gatherings. It was close to 11 P.M. when Jerome finally came home and after joining in the conversation for an hour, we all decided to call it a night, because Annie and Jerome had to get up early for work the following morning, and Bernie and I were driving up to Donegal, two hundred miles away.

I was looking forward to a good night's sleep because I had not slept on the plane the previous night on my flight across from the United States.

The house had a very odd layout: the kitchen and dining room was on the first floor; there were two bedrooms and a bathroom on the second floor; and there was a sitting room and a bedroom on the third floor.

We had spent the evening on the third floor sitting room and Annie had assigned me the small bedroom right next to the sitting room. Bernie, Jerome and Annie occupied the bedrooms on the second floor.

After everyone had gone down the stairs to their respective rooms, I lay in bed reading a book for almost an hour, a habit I acquired early in life. Then, I put out the light in the room and got into bed.

Almost immediately I felt a wave of uneasiness crawl over me. It was a vague sense of fear at first that had no particular focus but left me feeling very uncomfortable. I do not know how much time had passed before I first became aware of this nagging fear, but I do know that as the minutes ticked away the sense of fear gradually escalated, until it developed into a serious panic attack that had me scrambling out of the bed and groping for the light switch on the wall.

I was astounded by this assault on my senses and was convinced that there was somebody in the room who was threatening me.

But the minute the light went on I could see that there was no one in the room and the panic evaporated like smoke in a breeze, although I was left with a rapidly beating heart and a profound sense of embarrassment, because here I was a thirty-year-old behaving like a scared child.

I lay on the bed with the light on for about fifteen minutes until I had calmed down and got control of my scattered emotions. During that time I tried to make some sense of what had just happened, but the small tastefully decorated room gave me no clues on what might have provoked the panic. It was like a hundred other bedrooms I had slept in.

I stepped out of the bed again and cautiously opened the bedroom door and looked out into the hallway.

I could see little in the dim light and could not hear any sounds from the rest of the inhabitants of the house. I closed the door again and headed back to bed.

I lay there for some time trying to analyze what had happened, but I could come up with no explanation, so I switched out the light and went beneath the covers of the bed.

Almost immediately, the panic attack struck again, this time more intense than before, and when I could endure the terror any longer I jumped out of bed and put the light on again. The fear immediately subsided.

I was bewildered at what was happening to me because the experience seemed so irrational. There was nothing about this room that frightened me when the light was on, but when the light went out my senses were immediately assaulted.

I had been afraid of the dark when I was a child and at one time would not go to sleep unless there was a low light lit in the room. But even back then my fear was a vague unfocused experience and not at all like the acute terror I was experiencing in this room in Monkstown.

Needless to say I did not put the light out again and I lay in bed sleepless for the rest of the night, looking around apprehensively and waiting for something to happen, but nothing did. All was silent.

I was very glad when I heard Annie and Jerome moving around about 7AM, and delighted to get up and join them for breakfast.

I did not say anything to them about my night of fear, and I did not say anything to Bernie when he got up later. I was too embarrassed, because in the light of day I thought that my fear would have seemed childish to them. Besides I would have difficulty describing what had happened.

But in the months and years that followed I thought of Monkstown frequently, and the passage of time did not make my experience that night any less traumatic: I still thought it a very bizarre experience that I was unable to forget.

Two years later when I visited Annie and Jerome again, who were by this time living in London, I decided that I was going to question Annie about the room in Monkstown in the hope that she might provide me with some insights into the incident.

As soon as I got Annie alone in the sitting room I asked her to tell me what she knew about the room I had slept in while visiting her in Monkstown. I saw no point in beating around the bush because I really wanted an answer to the question.

"Why do you ask?" she said.

Again, I was very direct: "I had a bad experience there that night and I would like you to tell me what you know about this room. I told her I thought it is haunted. Then I told her what had happened.

Annie responded by saying that the house had the reputation of being haunted but she had never experienced anything unusual in the house and neither had most of the overnight guests she had entertained there over the years.

But then she went on to say that over the years she had lived there she had two other guests who had complained about this particular room, but she had dismissed their complaints because she knew that they were aware that the house had a reputation of being haunted, and she thought they were just trying to tease her.

"We were told that there were two suicides in this house, and because of this word got out the house is haunted.

"But we had not experienced anything there so we thought it was nonsense. Anyway we do not believe in ghosts. But it is odd that you sensed something. You did not know anything about the room's reputation."

When she said "the room's reputation" I got the chills.

"Are you saying the suicides took place in that room? And you never thought it important to let me know this?" I said, "You let me go in there without warning me?"

Annie and I then had our first and only fight. I was furious that she had not let me know about the room; she was furious because she thought I was behaving like a child.

"I thought you had more sense than that," she said

After a little while we calmed down and I never brought up the subject of Monkstown with her again. But I was still left with the experience and my confusion over it.

In the years since then I have come up with two theories about what might have provoked the panic attack, nether of which give me any closure on the matter.

The first theory is a quasi-scientific explanation that goes as follows:

Sometimes, when a person dies violently in a room, the walls of the room are impregnated with a barrage of atoms thrown off from the body as the victim struggles with death. This room remains impregnated with the violence of the death, and years later certain people who are sensitive to such things, like mediums, react adversely to the atmosphere of the room, just as I and a number of other people had at Monkstown, and they become convinced the room is haunted.

I have no proof that any of this is possible, but I know that there must be some explanation for what I experienced, and this theory makes sense if you accept the logic of the theory.

The second theory is far less complicated and is one that would be accepted by most Irish people who believe in God and ghosts.

This theory simply argues that the room is haunted by the suicides, and that I am one of those people who are sensitive to the presence of ghosts, even if I spend a great deal of energy rejecting the whole notion of ghosts.

Anyway, I have never been back to Monkstown and would not go there ever again for any reason. However, Monkstown, like the McLeod farm in South Donegal, has left me a legacy: it has planted seeds in my mind that prevent me from agreeing with the views of Annie and my friend Jim Doherty who argue that ghosts are a lot of nonsense and no one in their right mind should believe in them.

*

The third incident which has influenced my attitude towards the existence of ghosts had its origins back in 1951 and involved a niece of mine, Ena O'Neill. who claimed at that time that she was seeing ghosts in her family home in Dungloe, Co.Donegal. I did not believe her at the time, but forty years later while doing research for *Death in Templecrone,* my book on the Irish famine, I came across documents that suggested that there was some substance to her story after all.

I was in my late teens and Ena was about five years old the morning I learned for the first time that Ena had been seeing ghosts. I had visited my sister, Brigit Mary, Ena's mother, early one morning and Ena decided to accompany me back to my mother's house, which was located half a mile away.

On the way down the steep incline from Ena's home, Ena looked back and said: "They are out on the roof again, four of them this time, two men and a woman and a wee boy."

I looked back at the building she lived in but I could not see anything on the roof, so I asked her what she was talking about.

Ena stopped and looked back and then pointed at the roof: "Those people there all wrapped up in white sheets. There's four of them today."

Of course I could not see anybody on the roof, and I really did not know what to say to her about her imaginary friends.

So I told her we should keep on walking and not pay any attention to the people on the roof.

"That's what my mother says I should do. But they are there most mornings and I see them on my way to school."

When I got down to my own house I waited until Ena was not in the room and then I brought up with my mother the subject of the ghosts in the white sheets: I told her Ena was convinced that there were ghosts on the roof of her house and that they appeared to her every morning.

"I think Ena has a very weird imagination," I said. "She shouldn't talk like that or people will think she is crazy."

My mother's response surprised me.

"Ena's not off her head. Her mother had the priest visit that place twice. All of the family hear footsteps on the stairs at night. Opening and closing doors. Voices. Moans. But the priest could do nothing. I told her several times to leave the place. But she intends to move out of Dungloe in the next few months and she does not want to leave the house until she is ready to leave Dungloe."

I had known nothing about the ghosts, mainly because I had been away from home most of the time during the previous few years, and it was during this time that my sister had moved into the apartment and, according to her, inadvertently moved in with a community of poltergeists.

I felt like laughing, but didn't dare in case I offended my mother.

This occurred during a period of my life when I no longer believed in ghosts, banshees and other supernatural beings and considered them a lot of superstitious nonsense.

So it was easy for me to blame Ena's "hallucinations" on the fear generated by the rest of the family who were sometimes convinced that the apartment house was overrun with ghosts during the night, and who interpreted every creek of the old building as the footsteps of a poltergeist on the prowl.

Forty years passed before I thought of Ena's story again and when I did it was return with an immense amount of credibility and I was never again to question Ena's mental stability or the conviction of the O'Neill family that something was seriously wrong with the building.

I arrived at my revised view of Ena's story while conducting research for a book on the history of the famine of the 1840s in Northwest Donegal. My research into the potato famine experience was a long drawn out affair and involved combing the archives in Dublin for any documentation on the famine in that area. The archives that contained documentation were housed in several different locations in Dublin and it took a great deal of effort and several trips from the United States to Dublin before I was convinced that I had enough documentation to be able to relate the story.

To save time, I hired an Australian scholar who was living in Dublin to work with me researching and copying the relevant documents. We rarely read any document at all completely: if there was a reference at all to Northwest Donegal, we just copied it and I would read it later.

When we had researched the archives completely for the famine years – 1845-1850 – I took all the documents back to the United States, assembled them all in chronological order, and then methodically began to carefully study each document, 1,000 documents in all, in order to develop an understanding of how the famine years were experienced in Northwest Donegal. Then I began to write *Death in Templecrone.*

I had almost completed putting the documents in chronological order for 1848 when I came across three separate documents, which between them, put a focus back on Ena's ghost story, and these documents were so astounding that I read them several times not quite believing what I was reading.

The first document was a memorial from the local relief committee to the government in Dublin asking for the establishment of a fever hospital in Dungloe.

The memorial stated that the Glenties Hospital, sixteen miles from Dungloe, which served the Dungloe area, was full to capacity, and that the people of the Dungloe area were dying in droves from a variety of "fevers", including typhus, and a new facility in Dungloe was needed to treat them.

The second document was a report on the construction of the fever hospital at the Fair Hill, Dungloe, which seemed to be on or near the location where Ena O'Neill's apartment house stood a hundred years later. By the end of 1848 the hospital was nearing completion.

The third document, dated in 1849, and this was the one that astounded me, was a letter to the Editor published in the Derry Journal, a regional newspaper, which stated that the death from typhoid fever in Northwest Donegal was still very high.

The writer stated that he passed the Dungloe Fever Hospital every morning, and every morning he saw the bodies of men, woman and children, *wrapped in white sheets,* stacked outside the hospital ready for mass burial.

As I read this I remembered Ena's story about the men, women and children, wrapped in white sheets, standing on the roof looking down at her every morning, and I instantly made the connection between her story and the famine documents on the deaths in Dungloe.

First of all, it was evident to me that this fever hospital was located in the same general area where Ena's house stood a century later. I also knew that Ena could not have known about the fever hospital, because I had never heard of it before, even though I consider myself a local historian.

I was at a loss to explain the obvious connection between Ena's ghosts in white sheets and the description of the famine dead wrapped in white sheets. The chance of it being a coincidence seemed to be very remote.

In view of this, if I were to rule out the possibility of the supernatural, what possible explanation can there be for my niece seeing corpses in white sheets in an area where there actually had been corpses in white sheets more than 100 years prior to that?

Ena was married and living in Dublin at the time that I made the discovery in the documents and I called her up and told her about the documents that I had uncovered which seemed to confirm her story of long ago.

She was not in the least bit surprised and her only comment was that she knew all along they were ghosts.

In the years since I first discovered these documents I have developed an explanation for Ena's ghosts – the only explanation that would fit all the facts of the incident.

I believe that Ena exhibited psychic abilities as a child – the same type of psychic abilities exhibited by mediums who sometimes are hired by police departments in the United States to solve crimes when all else fails. American television shows frequently highlight programs where psychics are hired by the police to develop clues to a criminal's identity, and these psychics often have flashbacks in which they experience the crime being committed and are able to identify the perpetrator.

When Ena saw those "ghosts" in white sheets on the roof of her house she was tuning in to a tragedy that occurred in that area more than a hundred years prior to that. She did not know the meaning of what she saw, or why she was seeing them, but then back in the early 1950s the idea that someone could have psychic abilities was not taken seriously and there was no serious television documentaries that gave credence to such unusual abilities. So, in the 1950s I thought Ena's complaints about the ghosts a little weird and was not inclined to take them seriously at all.

Of course, my explanation for Ena's experience answers one question but raises other questions.

For instance, were the ghosts actually there on the roof, or were they merely being projected on the roof subconsciously by Ena.? Why were the ghosts "live" when Ena saw them, but were dead in the description printed in the *Derry Journal* in 1849.

And what about the building today – were the multiple tenants of the building hearing and seeing things just as the O'Neill Family did sixty years ago. I decided to find out.

I made a call to a long-time friend in Dungloe, Fonzie McCullough, who owned a television and computer rental and repair business, and asked him if he knew anything about the building on the Fair Hill area of Dungloe.

Fonzie's profession brought him into almost every house in the area at one time or another and if anyone was in a position to have information about this building it was probably him.

When I called him I did not tell him up front about Ena's experience in the building or my finding documents relating to the fever hospital because I did not want to prompt him in any way. I just asked him if he had heard any stories about anything unusual about the building that he might have heard. But I drew a blank, and the only information I got from him was that he knew the building had been built in the 1930s.

Then I asked him if he had ever heard about the building being haunted, and he said he had not. Then I told him the Ena story and all about the famine documents and he was very intrigued about the whole story.

Fonzie went on to say that he knew several people who had lived in the building over the years and if I were interested he would call them up and ask them about what it was like to live there. I said I would be delighted if he would do this for me but I warned him not to tell them the reason for his questions. If they knew the Ena story they might just elaborate on it, which would destroy the objectivity of the information. He assured me he would quiz them without giving any background information.

But, Fonzie's little investigation drew a blank, nobody he spoke to gave him any indication that they had ever heard of hauntings in connection with the building or anything negative about it at all.

Finally. I decided to call Mary Benoit, my niece, who was the third oldest of the eleven O'Neill children who had lived in the building with her sister Ena, in order to quiz her about her experience there. She gave me an earful. Mary, who lives in Bristol, Connecticut with her husband Dr. Kenny Benoit, a surgeon, said the house was overrun with ghosts and every member of the family had come in contact with them and was terrorized by them. She said Ena's claims were not the product of an overripe imagination, but were similar to incidents that all of them were exposed to at one time or another. After a year living there the family left for Dublin.

Mary said that one night while she was in bed she heard footsteps slowly descending the stairs from the top floor to the ground floor, and since she, as an ten-year-old, was considered the fearless member of the family, she got up and crept down the stairs to see who was prowling around. She found the front door locked and nobody in the kitchen, but she did find clothes that were hanging on a line above the fireplace on fire, and had she not extinguished the flames the entire house might have burned.

Mary said it was not unusual to have all the bed clothes suddenly whipped off a bed in the middle of the night, or to find clothes strewn around a room during the day. Then there was the opening and closing of doors, and the clatter of dishes down in the kitchen after midnight, as if the house had other occupants who made themselves at home after dark.

Because of all this, my sister Brigid Mary called in Dr. Molloy, the parish priest, on two occasions to bless the house in order to drive away whatever was bothering the family so much. But the priest's prayers had no effect and the parade of poltergeists went on until they left the place for good.

Given the fact that I had been unable to find another family who had a similar experience before or after the O'Neills were there, I wondered if all this poltergeist activity was not so much connected with the house, but rather with one of the O'Neills. There have been well documented cases both in Europe and the United States of houses being haunted by "ghosts" who moved furniture around, which on investigation turned out that all the activity whirled around a single member of the family, usually a girl in the 12-14 age range. It seems each child involved had developed unusual kinetic abilities that they were not aware of and the result was plates flying through the air and chairs being overturned. And when the child was removed from the house, the "hauntings" stopped.

There were two problems with this explanation for what had happened on the Fair Hill. First, there were no O'Neill girls of that age living in the house at that time. Mary, the oldest girl, was only ten. More importantly, there was the linkage between what Ena saw on the roof, and the famine documents which described a similar scene – indeed almost identical. This would suggest that there was a Famine connection to the poltergeists which for some unknown reason only the O'Neills were tapping into.

So, what is the final word on the story about Ena and the ghosts in white sheets? The truth is that there is no final word. It remains a bizarre little tale that offers no rational explanation. It remains a mystery.

MARY & JAMES CAMPBELL,
OWNERS OF CAMPBELL'S HOTEL -- 1920

THE IDIOT SAVANT

County Donegal, which is tucked up in the northwestern corner of the Irish Republic, was almost completely isolated from the rest of the Republic in the late 1940s. Donegal is part of the historic 9-county province of Ulster, but six of the counties are under British jurisdiction, and three of these six – Derry, Tyrone and Fermanagh – form a barricade between Donegal and the rest of the Republic, leaving it like an orphan tucked away in a corner. Only a two-mile wide strip of land united South Donegal with the other 25 counties of the Irish Republic.

Donegal has more in common with the six counties of British Ulster than it has with the counties of the Irish Republic. It has a similar religious and cultural mix, and it has two communities: one, which identifies itself as being Protestant of British origin; the other views itself as Irish Catholic.

In the 1940s, each community had many different traditions which they celebrated separately. They were interested in different sports, and they had entirely different views on political issues. But they had one thing in common: they had a common interest in music, theater, movies, literature and all types of entertainment.

Back in the 1940s, there were not that many options available for those who patronized entertainment events. A single new movie made the rounds of the small towns every few weeks; a touring theatrical company made the circuit every year; a circus came to the small villages every two years; and in between those events there might be a one-man show that featured a comedian or a fairly well known singer. Occasionally a juggler would appear, or a man named William McCann, who was billed as the man with the photographic mind. This story is about him.

I was completely amazed at the abilities of William McCann when I heard him perform on the stage of the Parochial Hall, Dungloe, in the late 1940s. Here was a person who was obviously of very limited intelligence – the intelligence of a two-year-old – and yet co-existing within this severely challenged intelligence were spectacular mental abilities far beyond the range of normal people. His ability to remember details from every single day of his life from the age of four was truly astounding. If given a date, he could instantly tell what day of the week it was; what the weather was like on that day. He could also describe the major stories that were published in the *Irish Times,* a national newspaper, on that particular day.

His phenomenal memory was something he was apparently born with, and so was ability to remember every day of his life. But the stories from the *Irish Times* was something his father had programmed into him from the age of four by reading the newspaper aloud to him every day. The boy absorbed every word every day and could recall every word thirty-one years later.

I first became aware of this unusual human being who was widely known as an idiot savant-- part idiot, part genius -- when a poster was put up in various locations around the town announcing the upcoming arrival of McCann to put on a show at the Parochial Hall. The poster gave many details about McCann's abilities, and I was skeptical about him at first because I thought that a combination of an idiot and a savant was too incredible to be true.

And I couldn't make up my mind whether the ability to remember what happened on every single day of one's life was an ability to be admired or an ability to be feared.

I was only fourteen at the time but I knew there were a number of days of my past life that I would much rather forget about so I would not like the ability to recall every tiny detail of these days at a moment's notice. But I was fascinated by the savant's gift, if you would call it a gift, and I was determined to go see his show when it arrived in Dungloe.

Early on the afternoon of the day of the show two men and a woman showed up at the front door of our hotel, and the older man asked my mother if they could book bed and breakfast for two nights. My mother said they could. The man then asked if they could have a room with two beds, as they all liked to sleep in the same room. My mother looked them over carefully, and when the woman saw the way they were being scrutinized, she said the younger man was her son and he couldn't sleep alone in a room because he got nightmares.

I took a careful look at the younger man, who was about thirty-five, and I came to the conclusion that he was a little strange, because he had a vacant look and he stood absolutely still, staring at the floor.

When my mother did not answer immediately, the woman spoke again: "We are here to put on a show in the Parochial Hall tonight -- my son has a photographic memory and he is here to show the people his gifts. Tomorrow night he will put on the show in Annagry, but we want to stay here tomorrow night, too, because we know this is the best place for us to stay."

My mother did not know why the woman thought our hotel was the best place of all the guesthouses in the area, but she was to learn the reason later in the day.

This was my introduction to William McCann and his family, and somehow I was very disappointed in him.

My mother agreed to keep the three of them at a price that was acceptable, and she told me to take a single bed out of another room and put it in our largest bedroom that already had a double bed.

When I went off to get the bed I noticed that the family was following me. "You must put the bed up the way our son William wants it," said Mrs. McCann. "You just can't throw it up any old way."

I said nothing, but I was getting irritated with the McCann trio. Somehow I had imagined that William McCann, the man with the photographic memory, would be a genius full of personality, but here was a man who remained completely silent, and looked like he had no personality at all.

As I was erecting the bed under the guidance of William – the bottom of the bed had to be lined up with the head of the double bed – and a large teddy bear had to be place on a table near his bed.

"Teddy is his friend," said Mrs. McCann.

"He is my best friend," said William.

The father suddenly turned to me and asked me my date of birth. I told him: January, 14, 1934.

The father then turned to William, and said: "William, tell him what kind of day the Fourteenth day of January, Nineteen Thirty-four was."

William answered instantly. "I got up at eight o'clock and put on my brown pants and brown pullover and brown shoes and I went down the stairs and Mammy gave me a boiled egg, porridge, toast and tea with no sugar in it. Sugar is bad for you it rots your teeth. That is the reason I never have it, and I never have any sweets either.

"It was raining outside and I knew that I would have to put on my brown raincoat when I went out to go to my school. Daddy then read me a whole lot of stories from the newspaper, twenty-four in all"

William then to went on to relate items of news that his father had read, much of it about Hitler, and I think he would have rambled on all day if his father had not interrupted him and told him that that would be enough. I was utterly astounded at the demonstration. I tried to ask William some questions but the mother would not let me. She said William did not like questions unless they came from his father, and then she asked me to leave because they were tired. So, I left and went in search of my father and found him serving customers in our bar.

I told him all about William and his amazing gift, but I also said he seemed very withdrawn and seemed to have little or no personality, and I was confused by him.

It seems my father had already heard about William when he visited Glenties, a nearby town, several years previously. He said McCann is what is called an idiot savant, someone who has some amazing mental capacity in some areas, but can be severely retarded in other areas. { In modern times such people are called autistic. }

"His special gift is that he can recall every detail of every day of his life. But all he knows is about what he saw or heard, and all he can do is repeat everything he saw or heard. He is not a genius and has low intelligence."

I asked my father how could anyone be sure that he was really remembering the past and not making it up. After all there was no way to check. But my father said he had been tested, and he was genuine.

And he said I could test him with an old newspaper that dated back to a week after I was born which he kept in a drawer upstairs. The newspaper had carried a story about the death of one of my father's aunts and that was the reason he had held on to it. I made a note of all the stories on the front page of *The Irish Times* and decided I was going to bring *The Irish Times* to the show and test McCann's abilities for myself.

The McCann family stayed in their room for more than an hour and then they came down and I met them in the front hallway. They wanted to get instructions on how to get to the Parochial Hall, which was down a lane from Carnmore Road, a side street. I gave them the instructions and as they were leaving the father came over to me and whispered "What Protestant Church do you go to? We are Presbyterians."

I was astounded by the question, mainly because I could not imagine why they thought I was a Protestant.

"I am not a Protestant." I said.   "I am a Catholic."

Now it was their turn to look astounded.

"We were told this is a Protestant house. You have a good Protestant name – Campbell."

"Well, we are not Protestant. And there are plenty of Campbells around here who are not Protestant either."

There was an awkward moment of silence and then they went off to see the Parochial Hall, and I went off to tell my mother that their guests had taken us for "good Protestants." My father and mother laughed at the mistake, because it had happened frequently, because visitors from Scotland who were touring Ireland were often attracted by the Campbell name – one of the most common names in Scotland – and stayed in our hotel rather than Sweeney's Hotel across the street, which they perceived to be an "Irish hotel."

Actually, the Sweeney name was also of Scottish origin – MacSwane – and the Sweeney family were our cousins.

I assumed the McCanns were from British Northern Ireland, where religious affiliation is so openly important, but when I checked the register I saw they were from the Republic, in East Donegal, an area with a considerable Protestant population.

I was caught off guard by the question for a number of reasons. First of all, while the people of Donegal at that time had the same sectarian tensions evident across the border in the north, they had learned not to express them openly, and so there was very little open conflict. We all had adopted a posture that everything was lovely in the garden, and a focused question about religion was just not done. I knew however that the error was not deliberate.

I wondered who told them we were Protestant. Was it somebody trying to embarrass them?

Mr. and Mrs. McCann acted a little embarrassed when they returned, but William had the same vacant look as if he was aware of nothing. My parents were friendly to them and acted as if they had heard nothing about their conversation with me. To put them at their ease, my mother who was very kind and generous, offered to provide them a free meal, consisting of boiled eggs, homemade bread and cheese. The McCann's accepted, but asked if William's eggs could be boiled for exactly three minutes, and if William could time the eggs being boiled, because he would not eat them if the were over or under three minutes. She also said William would rather toast than homemade bread and would like the bread toasted on one side only, with jam on the un-toasted side and butter on the toasted side.

She said William would also like to watch the toast being made, because few could make it right unless he supervised them. My mother agreed to all this, although I noticed that her face was getting a little red, a sure sign she was getting annoyed. In a fit of unusual generosity, my father offered the McCanns a free drink, Guinness for the men and port wine for Mrs. McCann, an offer that was coldly rejected by Mr. and Mrs. McCann, who said they never touched the stuff.

"Drink is the tool of the Devil," said William, making a rare contribution to the conversation.

My father retreated to the bar, and my mother headed for the kitchen with William in tow.

Several hours later, an hour before the show began, the McCanns headed off for the Parochial Hall, and I followed them forty-five minutes later. When I arrived there were quite a few curious people there who had already paid the one shilling admission fee, and the hall was three quarters full by the time the curtain went up.

William sat in a chair in the center of the stage looking straight ahead his face expressionless. His father stood beside him, looking a little nervous. His father opened the proceedings by saying that William had very unusual gifts: he had a photographic memory and could remember everything that had happened to him every day of his life. He could remember which day of the week that any particular date fell on and could remember what the weather was like. The father went on to say that they had read to William all the major stories in the *Irish Times* every day and he could remember every one of them.

Mr.McCann said the audience could ask about particular dates and they could ask about the news, or the weather, or about the day of the week this date fell on.

But no general questions of any kind were permitted.

After William answered a number of questions about particular dates, I decided to test him by asking about what he remembered about January 4, 1934, which was the date on the old newspaper that I had brought along.

William answered as follows: "I got up in the morning at three minutes to eight and put on my black suit, my black jersey and my black shoes and went down to breakfast. The sun was shining outside.

I had porridge, two boiled eggs, and one slice of brown bread with butter and jam. Then my father read seventeen stories from *The Irish Times.*"

He then went on to list the same stories that were in the paper I had, not missing one. At this point his father intervened and asked the audience for another question.

Several times during the show that followed members of the audience threw simple questions at William, which seemed to confuse him. Questions like "How did you feel when your father read the story about that terrible car accident," but the father always intervened, but not before the expression on William's face made it clear that he had no idea what these questions were about.

After a number of these incidents, I came to the conclusion that William was a little like a parrot that could play back all that was programmed into him, but had no understanding about the events he was describing and no feelings whatsoever about any of it. I thought it possible he had little feelings about anything. He was like a large filing cabinet that contained hundreds of files and countless thousands of pieces of information, but like the file cabinet, he had no understanding of any of this information.

The parents knew that William could not understand the nature of the information he had imprinted in his mind, and could only recall the information when, like a modern computer, he was given precise commands. If these commands were not precise, William reacted with confusion.

I was immensely curious about William's gift, and I wondered if he had total recall of any other type of information that he had not displayed at the show.

Twice during the evening the father had departed from his own rules: he showed the audience how William could recall every scene in a Western movie he saw, and was able to give a complete list of the credits of everyone involved in the movie.

Another time he gave a listing of all the train schedules in the Ulster rail system for the previous six months. It took ten minutes.

The audience responded positively to the show and William got a big ovation when the show was over.

After the show ended, William was hurried out of the hall by his parents and he was quickly guided back to our house, where they retreated to their room, no doubt to review the show and count the takings.

Later, they came down to the kitchen and asked if William could listen to a program on Radio Luxembourg that played all the top songs of the week. The program began at 11pm and ran for an hour. My mother said he could, but that she was going to bed. My father went to bed with her, and shortly after that the McCanns went to bed leaving me and William sitting listening to the top hit songs.

My curiosity about William's gift prompted me to probe his mind a little now that his parents weren't around. I wanted to see how much he knew about the world around him. At the time, I did not see anything wrong with this.

I asked him if he knew who Eamon De Valera was; DeValera was the Irish political leader in the Republic at the time. He said he did not. I tried a new approach: I asked him who the head of the government was and he said Basil Brooke. I told him he was wrong – that Basil Brooke was the leader in Northern Ireland – and the correct answer was Eamon DeValera, since he and his parents lived in an area controlled by the Southern Government. He looked at me blankly as if he did not understand me.

I asked him who he thought was the greatest person that ever lived and he said "King Billy," the seventeenth century British King who was the hero of the Ulster Orangemen. I asked if he knew who Patrick Sarsfield or Brian Boru, or Kevin Barry was, all of them heroes of the Irish Catholics. He said no. Then I told him that they were real Irish heroes, not a foreigner like King Billy. He got very upset at that and left the room.

A few minutes later his parents came down obviously furious and they began to shout at me for "interfering with the boy's mind". They asked what right did I think I had to be telling "the boy" a pack of lies that he did not want to hear. I remained silent throughout the tirade mainly because I did not know how to respond.

My parents heard the uproar and arrived on the scene to see what was going on, and when they found out they apologized to the McCanns and read the riot act to me. I said nothing and went off to bed.

But the row did not end there. When I got up the following morning, my mother was still furious at me because the McCanns had moved out and had gone looking for other accommodations. She said the McCanns had said I was trying to fill their son's head with Catholic propaganda and that I obviously hated Protestants.

I tried to defend myself by saying that William thought Basil Brooke was the leader of the whole country and all I was doing was pointing out an error to him.

But she said it was none of my business who he thought was leader of the country, and if he thought the King of Siam was the Irish leader it still was none of my business.

"His parents are filling his head with British propaganda," I said. "It is not right."

"Your father fills your head with rebel propaganda all the time, and that is not right either. He is not God. He can be wrong too. You had no right to be trying to tell that simple-minded person what to think, and his parents had every right to be angry with you."

I did not argue with her. My father never argued with her: he just listened to her and then walked away. He was a wise man, and I learned from him.

The McCanns never stayed in our hotel again, although they were back in Dungloe several times in the years that followed. I always went to see the performance, even though it did not change from the show I heard the first time. But my fascination with a mind that such immense abilities and such immense disabilities continued to fascinate me, and still does.

Donegal is very different now than it was back in the 1940s. Sectarianism has retreated deeper beneath the surface, even though it is alive and vigorous across the border in some areas. The arts still remains the great common denominator, and television brings integrated shows into all of Ulster homes. Still there are Catholics living deep inside Protestant Belfast who reject all things British, and Protestants living in East Donegal who still believe King Billy was the greatest man who ever lived. Some things never change.

STORIES ABOUT THE OLD RECTORY

There are a score of ancient buildings in northwest Donegal that have a history dating back for centuries. Some of these, like Sweeney's Hotel in Dungloe, have been in the same family since the middle of the 18th Century, while another, in Maghery, was the home of a 17th Century landlord and is still in very good condition. Many other mansions, which were the homes of British landlords, are in ruins, and their former owners are all but forgotten by most of the people who live near them.

These ancient structures witnessed the endless conflicts between the inhabitants of the area and the representatives of the British Government who imposed British rule on a mainly Irish Catholic population, the majority of whom spoke only Gaelic until the middle of the 19th Century.

Although the Rebellion of 1798 had little impact on the area, two famous rebels Wolfe Tone and Napper Tandy visited the area during the rebellion. Napper Tandy landed in Burtonport with a consignment of arms and ammunition for the rebels, and Wolfe Tone fought with the French Navy in a battle with the British Navy off the northwest coast.

The great Irish famine of the 1840s had a tremendous impact on the area, killing thousands and forcing thousands more to immigrate to America. A number of the leaders of the Irish rebellion of 1916-1921 were natives of the region.

Throughout all this period these ancient structures witnessed the tide of battle during rebellions, and the catastrophic fatalities during the famine years.

Among the buildings with the most colorful history in the area is a large mansion known as the Old Rectory, at Maghery. In the pages that follow, are a number of tales connected with this ancient mansion, some related by my father and other local storytellers; other gathered from the National Archives in Dublin.

1…. MY FATHER'S STORY

The first time I saw the Old Rectory, which squats on a 20-acre plot of land near the beach, I was visiting the area with my father. I thought that this gloomy structure had all the characteristics of the haunted houses I had seen in some of the boys' adventure comic books I had in my collection at home, because of its massive gray walls, gray roof, and windows that also seemed gray.

I asked my father if he knew who owned the building and if anyone was living there, because it had that abandoned look that was typical of the deserted houses I had seen in the area. He said it had not been occupied in many years and that it was a 150-year old rectory owned by the Protestant Church of Ireland.

My father and I were sitting on a blanket near the beach and we had a clear view of the Old Rectory and of all the other points of interest in the surrounding area. It was a beautiful summer day and my father had taken me to Maghery from our home in Dungloe six miles away. Dungloe did not have a good beach of its own.

My father was a compulsive story teller and once he saw I was interested in the Old Rectory he began to tell me stories about it. My father could tell stories about almost every building in the parish and all that was needed to get him going was to ask a question about a building. Sometimes I liked those stories, but at other times I thought many of them boring. But I welcomed his stories about the Old Rectory because the building had such a spooky appearance and I thought it was bound to have very interesting stories connected with it.

My father began his description of the Old Rectory by asking me a question.

"Do you see those huge twelve-foot walls that are over there at the far end of the beach? The ones that are three or four feet thick? "

I said I did. Indeed: it would be very hard to miss the walls because they were a major part of the scenery, and like the rectory, they were a huge gray heap that attracted your attention.

"Well, the rector who lived in the rectory during the great famine more than a hundred years ago built those walls around his own land with money he was given by the government to feed the people who were dying of hunger. He hired men women and children to carry rocks from the shore to build the walls, and some of the workers were so sick they could barely walk. And if they couldn't work they got no money to buy food, and so they died."

I thought this was a terrible story and I thought that if the rector had been a good Christian he would have given the people the money directly and not made them work for it.

As I looked at the walls I thought that they seemed unnaturally tall and unnaturally wide.

I asked my father why the walls were so tall and so wide, and he told me that the rector wanted to protect his sheep and cows from the hungry people so he made sure that the people would have great difficulty getting to them.

"Not one of his animals was ever stolen during the famine," my father said.

I asked my father what happened to the rector after the famine was over and he said that he was transferred out of the area to another part of Donegal.

My father then went on to tell me about another rector who lived in the Old Rectory and who also became well known for conduct that that brought disgrace to him and his family.

"This happened ninety years after the famine. This rector ran off with a Catholic girl from this area and both of them disappeared and were never heard of again. It was the worst scandal that ever happened around here."

I was only seven years old when my father told me this but even then I knew that Catholics and Protestants living in the area at the time would think this was a terrible thing: Protestants and Catholics just did not marry one another, ever, and the fact that the Protestant involved was a clergyman made matters a hundred times worse.

"Some say they never left the area at all and were done away with once it became known that they were doing wrong things, and they are buried up there in the bogs somewhere, or were thrown into a lake. I don't know if this is true: nobody knows except the pair of them, or the people who might have done away with them. They say their ghosts haunt the rectory. "

My father then went on to tell me that every Protestant Rector who lived there was considered one of the most important personalities in the parish, and along with the landlord and his agent wielded the most power. He said the landlord and the rector were considered "gentlemen," but no Catholic in the area, no matter what their wealth, were ever considered gentlemen. My father said that his great uncle, Johndy Sweeney, owned a hotel in Dungloe during the famine and could be considered rich, but no member of the British administration would ever have considered Sweeney a gentleman, simply because he was a Catholic.

The Old Rectory was considered one of the most important structures in the whole parish because of the power of those who lived there.

"During the time the British occupied this part of Ireland the Catholic people had to support the rector by giving him ten percent of their income. The Rector also owned most of the land around Maghery and collected rents from tenants. These rectors were very well off."

The Protestants population was only 7% of the entire parish, yet all the land was in the hands of Protestant landlords and clergy, and no Catholic occupied any position of prominence in the parish until the late nineteenth century, long after the Great Famine.

My father did not view the Old Rectory as a building with religious connections: he viewed as a symbol of British authority that was no longer in effect in this part of Ireland.

The last story my father told me was about a time he visited Maghery in the 1880s, when he was a teenager. He said he and a friend had come out to Maghery to swim and sit around the beach on a Sunday afternoon, and while he was there numerous elegant horse-drawn carriages arrived at the rectory, each carrying two or more beautifully dressed men, women and children. Some of the men were in the military uniform of the British Army.

Before the guests arrived, tables and chairs had been set up around the spacious well-kept grounds of the rectory and soon all were filled up as the guests settled in to an afternoon lunch hosted by the rector.

My father recognized some of the guests who were members of a landlord's family who lived at Roshine Lodge, Burtonport.

He also recognized a few others who were among the Protestant gentry in Gweedore. All had the demeanor and self-confidence of a privileged class of people, and none was Catholic.

During the afternoon many of these visitors came out of the rectory dressed in elegant clothing and strolled along the beach. Among them were young people of my father's age who completely ignored him as if he did not exist. That annoyed my father.

He said these people were representatives of the privileged minority in Northwest Donegal, who acted as they were a superior race and had no need to even look at those who supported them with their rents, or worked for them on their estates.

In later years my father came to the conclusion that the local Catholics were just as much to blame for the arrogance of these people as the people themselves. He said all the Catholics on the beach were deferential to this landlord class and this only reinforced their conviction that they were a chosen people.

The Old Rectory lost much of its social importance at the end of the nineteenth century when the British government forced many of the landlords to sell their property to their tenants, and after the Irish War of Independence, the landlords left the area and the Old Rectory became just a clergymen's residence and nothing more.

I passed the Old Rectory many times in the years that followed, but did not pay much attention to it. I was a regular visitor to Maghery beach and it was the sand and the sea that interested me not that old gray building..

Sometimes I glanced at the rectory and wondered about all the people who had lived there over the centuries, but I never once thought of entering the grounds and looking in the windows or of finding out who owned the building. I just was not interested. I felt I knew all that I need to know about the place and really was not interested in learning any more.

2.... *JOHN McCARTHY'S STORY*

In 1993, after I had published my first book, *A Molly Maguire Story,* I came back to Dungloe on vacation from the United States, and while there visited Delia O'Donnell, an old friend of the family, who had a house on Main Street, Dungloe. While I was there Delia told me that John McCarthy, a well-known American author, owned a house in the area and that he wanted to meet me because he had read my book. Delia went on to say that McCarthy had married a woman with local connections and that he was living in the Old Rectory in Maghery. As soon as I heard the Old Rectory mentioned I thought it would be interesting to go out there and meet him and see the inside of the rectory.

Ironically enough I had reviewed both of McCarthy's books for the *Irish Echo Newspaper,* a New York weekly and had given them good reviews. The books are entitled *The Best of Irish Wit and Wisdom* and *The Home Book of Irish Humor,* both of which sold very well in the United States.

A native New Yorker, McCarthy was a career journalist who had contributed columns to a number of newspapers including *The Irish Times,* a Dublin-based Irish daily newspaper. McCarthy was in retirement when he decided to buy the Old Rectory.

The Rectory, Maghery. Residence of the
Reverend Valentine Pole Griffith.

Church of Ireland Chapel (Protestant), Dungloe.

As we approached the Old Rectory I saw that it had not changed in appearance from the time I had first seen it as a boy. It was still the large gray building with the gray slate roof. When Delia and I arrived at the Old Rectory, it seemed at first that it was in total darkness, but then we noticed a candle flickering in one of the ground floor windows, so we knew someone had to be home. We knocked on the door and waited to be admitted.

The McCarthys greeted us warmly when we entered the front hallway, which was in total darkness, and escorted us into a living room that was full of antique furniture and was lit by a solitary candle.

I asked them if they had lost electric power, but John said they had not – that they had never turned the electric power on when they first moved in -- they preferred candle light because it gives the house a "cozy atmosphere".

"We do not even believe in lamps, although we do have some that we light in the bedrooms when we have overnight guests." he said. "Lamps are too modern and do not go with the house either."

John McCarthy was a great storyteller and he was a very entertaining host. While his wife made the ritual cup of tea and scones, John gave me his reasons why he had settled down in this isolated community, far from the bright lights of New York and Dublin.

"What I like most about this place is the absolute silence. You rarely hear a sound from the outside. Few beeping horns, no loud conversation. I can read and write without being disturbed. I did not know that I had been living in a very noisy world until I moved here.

McCarthy went on to describe his career as a journalist in New York and Dublin, and he talked for more than an hour describing the people he had met and the celebrities he had written about. In a way he reminded me of my father because he had a story for every occasion.

At one point the door to the living room swung open several inches creaking slightly as it opened. McCarthy stopped his storytelling, turned to his wife, and said: "See, there it goes again, it opens by itself.

Then he turned to me and said: "I think we got a ghost in the house, but she just laughs at me and says it is a writer's imagination."

I was inclined to agree with his wife but I did not say so. I had been living in a large Victorian house in Jersey City, New Jersey, for a number of years and was well used to doors opening and closing by themselves and never once did I attribute any of these happenings to a ghost, because I knew old houses were draughty structures full of strong air currents that could easily open and close doors. But I said nothing of this to the McCarthys.

I asked John McCarthy if he thought the place was haunted and he said that it definitely was.

"There is a woman in a white dress flitting around this place at night. I have seen her several times myself, but my wife thinks I am only seeing flashes of light from a passing car. But I know this is not what it is."

McCarthy went on to say that he wanted to move into the rectory in the first place because many local people said the rectory was haunted and he thought it would be fun to live in a haunted mansion, but he had been disappointed by the experience.

"I get no thrills. In the daytime this is a nice place. It has big windows and the light pours in from all directions. It is sort of cheerful. But at night it has a strange atmosphere – an atmosphere I cannot define. It is just strange. But in spite of everything I still like the place and do not want to leave."

I thought a lot of his problems would be solved if he got the electricity turned on and lit up the house with bright lights. The flickering candlelight cast shadows and gave the room a spooky look.

At one point I had to go to the bathroom, so he lit another candle and took me out into the hallway and pointed up the stairs to the second floor. "There is a toilet up there," he said and handed me the candle.

I climbed the stairs with the cocoon of light surrounding me and the shadows dancing up and down the stairs before and after me. It was a weird experience, like out of a ghost movie. It was hard to see the layout of the second floor, but I found the toilet.

As the night wore on I decided I did not like the atmosphere either and I also thought it strange, but I thought that my reaction to the place was based on the spooky light thrown by the candles and the dark shadows lurking around every corner.

"I suppose my main attraction to this place is based on its age – two hundred years old, said John. "Can you imagine the number of people who have lived here over the centuries and the tales these walls could tell if they could only speak?"

"When I first moved in here I thought I would in some way tune into the many generations of people who have lived here. I thought that they would have left something of themselves behind in the atmosphere of the place."

"But I sense nothing of the past. Nothing at all. But I think that ghost woman I am seeing was somebody who lived here and this is her spirit."

I mentioned to him the story my father had told me about the rector who had run off with the Catholic girl, but he dismissed the Catholic girl as a candidate. He said the couple had been seen in Australia and so the story was a love story not a crime story. He said they are probably still living out in Australia. I did not argue with him because I did not know what had happened to the rector and the love of his life.

I then told him the story about how my father had visited Maghery one summer day when he was a teenager and the rector was hosting a party, and I gave him my father's description of the guests and how they behaved.

'Well, the Anglo-Irish had a lot of class," he said. "You got to give them credit for that. There is not too much class around here any more. It is all gone with the wind."

In spite of his American birth, I thought McCarthy had inherited more than a little of the Irish trait of looking up to the "gentry." I believed Anglo-Irish gentry had won their place in the sun as a result of a military conquest, and they had lost it in the same manner during the Irish War of Independence.

I spent a long winter's evening with the McCarthy's and enjoyed their company. I was glad I had finally seen the inside of the Old Rectory, but I was not very impressed by it and was repelled by that vague feeling of uneasiness that I had experienced during my visit.

I had no plans ever to return there.

3...THE VALENTINE POLE GRIFFTH STORY

In 1993 I began research into the Famine experience in Northwest Donegal to gather material for a book later published in 1995 entitled *Death in Templecrone.* Templecrone is the parish in Northwest Donegal, which includes Maghery, Dungloe, Burtonport and a score of other settlements that was the subject of my famine study. The Famine material were scattered throughout Dublin in a number of different archives.

I was surprised at the extent and variety of information that the archives revealed – information that seemed to be unknown to the people who inhabited the parish of Templecrone in the late twentieth century.

Among this information was a portrait of Valentine Pole Griffith, the rector who lived in the Old Rectory during the 1840s at the height of the famine. The Rev Griffith owned several hundred acres of land around the Old Rectory, and he was noted for treating his tenants fairly. During the famine, he emerged from the archives as a tireless champion of the destitute Catholic population in the parish and who saved countless lives by raising money to feed the hungry after the British government failed in its responsibilities to the poor.

This favorable portrait of the Rev. Griffith was in contrast to the portrait of him handed down to me by my father who thought the rector had misused government money for his own use. Nothing could have been further from the truth.

Immediately after the first massive potato failure in 1845, the Rev Griffith organized a relief committee to raise funds that were used to compensate those who lost part of or all of their entire crop to the blight that had attacked the potatoes.

The Old Rectory became the headquarters for the relief effort over the next five years and the rector was relentless in his pursuit of funds for the people of Templecrone, writing a barrage of letters to the government in Dublin seeking help and contacting every charitable agency in Ireland and Britain for donations. He also traveled to Belfast to seek donations from wealthy Protestant businessmen.

Griffith was joined in his efforts by Francis Forster, a small landlord who lived in Burtonport, ten miles around the coastline from Maghery.

Between the two of them they did not leave a stone unturned in their efforts to keep the people of Templecrone from starving to death.

The Marquis of Connyngham, the Anglo-Irish aristocrat who owned 85% of the land in the area, was asked to get involved in the relief effort but he refused. Connyngham lived in Slane Castle outside Dublin, and he cared little for the welfare of his tenants. He visited his Templecrone estate only once in his lifetime.

Griffith and Forster demanded that the British Government ship free grain to the area, but the government refused to do this.

Instead the Government offered to loan money to local landlords that would be used for public works projects, and the landlords could then create projects and hire destitute people to work on them.

The money earned in this way could be used to buy food. The money, of course, had to be paid back by the landlords to the British government.

Neither Forster nor Griffith needed any work done on their estates, but they co-signed for loans anyway in order to get the money to feed their tenants. Forster build roads that did not go anywhere just to keep tenants working; the Rev Griffith built the massive walls around his estate in Maghery that served no useful purpose at all. The government had inspectors in the area whose job it was to see that all work was legitimate, but they turned a blind eye to the projects.

The efforts of both men might have enabled the inhabitants of Templecrone to survive the potato failure if the failure had been confined to just one year, but the crops failed on several years, and epidemics of disease swept over the area killing thousands who were weakened by hunger.

Through all these terrible years between 1845 and 1850, the Rev Griffith continued with his fund-raising activities and continued to get outside charitable organizations interested in the plight of the residents of northwest Donegal.

Prominent Quakers and representatives of Belfast relief organizations came to stay at the Old Rectory and were given a tour of the parish by the Rev Griffith.

Among these was the English-born Quaker William Bennett, who stayed for a few days in Maghery in March 1847 with the Rev Griffith.

On March 23, Bennett had seen men, women and children eating grass and seaweed near Dungloe and he was appalled that this should be happening in the United Kingdom, which was then the richest country in the world.

Bennett commented bitterly that the Irish were citizens of the United Kingdom and that they should be treated with the same compassion that citizens in England would be treated if they were in similar circumstances.

And he said England was responsible for the situation and morally bound to come to the aid of the Irish, because London claimed jurisdiction over the Irish and were therefore responsible for their welfare.

In one letter, Rev. Griffith wondered if there was a hidden agenda in London's failure to do its duty, a thought that might have been planted in his mind by the opinion of many Irish leaders that London was out to destroy the Irish nation, because the government seemed indifferent to the mounting casualties.

Griffith put his family at risk by continuously interacting with the sick and dying people who came to the soup kitchens he had established in Maghery and Dungloe to distribute food to the needy. His wife and daughters worked with him on these projects and were exposed to the typhus and cholera that had raged like wildfire through the parish.

But he and his family survived the famine and in the 1850s moved to a new parish in South Donegal.

The sad aspect of the great service that the Rev Griffith had provided to the inhabitants of Templecrone in their hour of need was that his good deeds were not remembered by the generations that followed.

Somehow the memory died with the end of the famine and all that my father, who was born two generations after the famine, knew about him was that he had built the famine walls at Maghery with government money. Nothing else.

4   ASENATH NICHOLSON AND THE OLD RECTORY

Francis Forster and the Rev Valentine Griffith were not the only landlords in Templecrone. The Marquis of Conyngham owned more than 85% of the real estate in the parish, but unlike Forster and Griffith he absolutely refused to get involved in famine relief at all. Conyngham's tenants were told to save themselves, and were it not for the efforts of Forster and Griffith all of Conyngham's tenants might have starved.

Forster was furious at Conyngham for not pulling his weight in Templecrone because he had left the entire responsibility for famine relief on the shoulders of him and Griffith.

Conyngham was unmoved by Forster's rage. A close friend of the Royal Family, the Marquis was above the law and beyond shame.

But even though Forster could not force Conyngham to help his tenants, he found other ways to harass and embarrass the landlord and make his society friends in London know how he was treating his tenants.

One of Forster's tactics was to invite a reporter from the *Times* of London into Templecrone to see first hand the horrors that were taking place on the Conyngham estate. This reporter wrote an expose that must have infuriated Conyngham.

Another tactic was to invite Asenath Nicholson to Donegal. She was an American evangelist and reformer who had spent a great deal of time in Ireland before and during the famine preaching the gospel and feeding the poor. Nicholson was well known on both sides of the Atlantic.

Nicholson was a fearless advocate for the downtrodden I and she was openly critical of slavery in the United States and British policies towards the Irish, who she considered to be just as badly off as the American slaves.

By inviting Nicholson to Donegal in 1847 Forster knew that Nicholson would be appalled at the condition of the tenants in the parish and would have no hesitation in speaking out about what she had witnessed. He hoped that the publicity that she generated would focus on the plight of the people of the parish and would shame Conyngham into getting involved in famine relief.

Nicholson arrived in Burtonport and stayed the first night with Forster in Roshine Lodge, and she was shocked at the utter desolation she saw on her way into the parish.

The next day she went to Maghery to visit Rev.Griffith and she was appalled at the destitution in the countryside from Burtonport to the Old Rectory. Griffith and his family had a huge urn and they made a hundred gallons of soup every day and distributed it to people who were dying of hunger and disease.

The Rector told him that the local Catholics were leaving dead bodies at the rectory door every night because they could not transport the bodies to Dungloe for a Catholic burial and they knew the rector would provide a decent Christian burial for their relatives. Griffith did this and buried the bodies near the Protestant Graveyard in nearby Termon.

Griffith also brought Nicholson into Aranmore Island, the hardest hit area of Templecrone and exposed her to the horrors of the widespread disease and high mortality among the island population.

One of the most gruesome aspects of her visit to the island is described in *Lights and Shades of Ireland* the book she published in 1850. In the book, she describes how the island had well nourished dogs who acquired this condition from feeding on corpses they dragged out of shallow graves.

Nicholson left the island furious at the system of government that left people in this plight and determined to bring the situation in Ireland to the attention of the world.

She was also deeply impressed by the Rev Griffith and his family and their struggle to keep their Catholic neighbors alive. She believed that the Rev Griffith was a true Christian.

After she left Templecrone, she went to Gweedore, the parish north of Templecrone and found a similar situation there, in spite of the fact that a self-promoting landlord named George Hill was claiming that all was well in the parish.

In the years that followed Nicholson continued to advocate reforms in Ireland and raise funds for Irish famine relief, and she remained in the public eye, both in Europe and in the United States until the early 1850s, when ill health made her retreat to Jersey City, NJ, where she died on May 15, 1855, from typhoid fever.

Until her death she continued to correspond with the Rev Valentine Pole Griffith in the Old Rectory and learned from him in 1849 that 500 had died in Aranmore up to this point from hunger and disease.

It was remarkable that the Rev Griffith never contracted typhoid fever in Ireland during all those years that he was exposed to the disease on a daily basis. And it was ironic that Asenath Nicholson should die of the disease in Jersey City, long after she escaped from disease- ridden Donegal.

Nicholson's funeral services were held on May 16, 1855 in the Dutch Reformed Church, Erie and Third Street, Jersey City. The Rev Strong, her close friend gave the eulogy.

Meanwhile, the Old Rectory continues to stand guard near the beach at Maghery, gray and silent. It has a new owner now, a retired schoolteacher named Dennis Hanlon who has been attempting to get the Old Rectory totally refurbished with government assistance. One would imagine that given the remarkable history of this place, especially during the famine, that he would get a great deal of support, but this is not the case, as there seems little interest in preserving a historic building like this. But Hanlon is pushing ahead anyway, in spite of official indifference and problems with teenagers who have committed vandalism in the building.

A few of the stories connected with the rectory have been related here, but I am sure there are hundreds of other stories about the Old Rectory that have yet to be told.

MANIAC

The cats and dogs that I have encountered over a lifetime have had a wide variety of personalities. Some were very affectionate; some were notable for their hostility; others seemed totally indifferent to human beings. Only a few displayed a high degree of intelligence, and very rarely did I come across an animal that seemed to have an intelligence that was almost human.

My sister Brigid Mary once had a dog named Spot who was one of those unusual animals. One Summer, while my sister was driving to Dublin she lost Spot in a town one hundred miles from Donegal. The family had gone into a restaurant for lunch and when they came back out Spot was no longer in the car. He had either opened the door himself or someone else opened the door to pet him, and Spot took off. The family spent the rest of the day looking for Spot, but they could not find him anywhere.

Four weeks later Spot arrived back in Donegal, having crossed mountain passes, made his way through deep glens, and fording rivers until he arrived thin and bedraggled at our door.

How did he do it? I do not know!

Then there was a cat named Maniac. The first time I met Maniac I knew I was being introduced to a very unusual cat. Cold green eyes stared at me from an elegant Persian body draped with long black fur. The stare I received was both arrogant and hostile, and he gave every indication that he did not like me at all.

I had never met a cat like that before. Apart from his exotic appearance, he seemed to have an air of bored sophistication about him and a low tolerance for young people like me who wandered into his domain.

As I was growing up, we had many cats as house pets, and so had my friends and neighbors, but all of them behaved as cats are supposed to behave: they ate, slept, and occasionally responded to human affection by purring. But I had never met a cat like Maniac before who seemed almost human in his ability to project a variety of emotions.

When I met Maniac I was sixteen and a student at St. Eunan's High School in Letterkenny. I became aware of the cat's existence from listening to a classmate named Brian Curran who was forever talking about the weird cat his Aunt Jane owned..

I thought Curran was a little bit odd because he talked about the cat all the time. Other boys talked about sports or about girls but all Curran talked about was this cat. In a way my first impression of Curran was that he was not just a little odd, but that he was in fact a little off center.

At first, I paid little attention to Curran's ramblings about the cat he called Maniac.

But after a time curiosity got the better of me and I asked Brian if I could visit his aunt, who lived a short distance from the school, so I could meet Maniac.

Curran turned me down initially, because he said Aunt Jane did not like visitors, and Maniac did not like visitors either, and he had no intention in bringing me to a house where I would get a very cold welcome.

But I persisted in pressing him for an invitation to meet the cat and in the end he agreed to take me down during our lunch break from school.

Curran seemed very nervous as we went down the street towards his aunt's house. There were times when I thought he was going to turn around and go back to the school.

As we approached the house, Curran told me that there were conditions attached to the visit: the visit would last no more than ten minutes and that I would agree to a whole set of rules that he would impose on me. I agreed to do whatever he asked.

He laid out the rules as follows: I was not to ask his aunt the meaning of the cat's name. I was not to ask where the cat came from. I was not to make any comments at all about the cat's personality. I was not to stare at the cat, and above all, I was not to try and pet him, unless I wanted to lose a few fingers.

However, Brian then decided to disobey the rules himself by giving me some background information on Maniac before we arrived at the house. I don't know the reason why he did that.

According to Curran, Maniac and a second kitten named Dipso had been given to his aunt by a gentleman admirer named McCauley who was inspired to name the kittens after an affliction he suffered from: alcoholism. Before this gentleman died, he used to say when he was a little drunk: "I am a dipsomaniac and I cannot do anything about it."

So, it was McCauley who named the kittens Dipso and Maniac.

Joe McCauley lived with his mother and a fat bedraggled cat that didn't like McCauley but loved his mother. When the cat got pregnant and gave birth to two kittens, McCauley's mother put the kittens in a cloth bag and tied the top and then told Joe to throw the bag in the river. Mrs. McCauley tolerated one cat around the house but she had no intention of putting up with three of them.

Joe had a soft heart and he could not bring himself to drowning the kittens.

So, instead he brought them to Aunt Jane as a "gift." Aunt Jane had a soft heart too and she gave them a home, a move she was to regret for years.

The two kittens were completely different from one another. Dipso was always giving affection to anyone who petted him; Maniac kept everyone except Aunt Jane at arm's length and scratched anyone who tried to fondle him. He even terrorized small dogs in the neighborhood which he attacked without provocation. He left the big dogs alone.

Apparently McCauley used to tell Aunt Jane that the personality of the cats was a result of the trauma they experienced when Mrs. McCauley handed them over to him for execution.

It was his opinion that cats were as perceptive as humans and were aware when they were in mortal danger. Dipso handled the traumatic experience by making love to everyone he met so no one would think of drowning him; Maniac reacted by spitting at everyone he met and only trusted the one person who gave him shelter – Aunt Jane.

But Brian said that Aunt Jane seemed to have more affection for the agreeable Dipso than she had for Maniac.

She made the mistake of making it obvious, something that infuriated Maniac, and he reacted by beating up Dipso almost every day. He hated Dipso and started a long campaign to get rid of him.

As I listened to this I became convinced that Curran was definitely off. I mean how could he possibly know what was in the cat's mind? How could he attribute any motivation to any of the cat's actions? Was he able to read the mind of cats? I began to think that I might have made a mistake of getting involved with Curran.

MANIAC

Curran must have sensed what I was thinking, or maybe the expression on my face gave me away, because he said he knew I did not believe him. "But just you wait," he said. "You will see for yourself."

Curran then continued his description of Maniac. "Maniac then started to lead the pliable Dipso out into the parts of Letterkenny that were a long way from his home, hoping no doubt to lose him, but Dipso always found his way back to Aunt Jane, no matter how far from home he had gone."

In the end, Dipso just disappeared, although not entirely without a trace: there were pieces of fur out in the back yard that were of the same type of white fur worn by the missing Dipso.

"I think Maniac killed and ate him," said Brian, as we arrived at the door of Aunt Jane's house. "He solved the Dipso problem permanently."

I started to laugh when he told me that, because I thought it absurd that one cat would murder another one over the love of a woman, but I stopped laughing when Brian got furious at me.

"You don't know this cat. He is evil. He can read your mind, so you better watch what you are thinking when you go inside or you will regret it."

At this point I did not know how weird the cat was but I certainly was convinced that Brian had a few squirrels in his attic, and they were interfering with his ability to reason. However, when Aunt Jane opened the door and stood there with this elegant, hostile cat by her side that looked at me contemptuously with those cold green eyes, I became a little uneasy for the first time and the thought occurred to me that maybe I should not have asked Brian to bring me there at all.

Aunt Jane was a little surprised to see us and she asked Brian what he wanted. Brian said he needed a book on Irish history to study for an exam he would be taking the following week and he said he wanted to borrow a book from Jane's library. She stepped to one side to allow us in and Brian walked inside, but before I could follow him the cat moved to the middle of the doorway, blocking me from going forward. He then crouched there glaring at me as if he were ready to launch an attack at any moment, and slowly began to swish his tail in a threatening manner.

I told Brian that I would wait outside for him, but Aunt Jane, who seemed embarrassed by the cat's antics, would not hear of it and she picked up the cat and waved me into the house. I went in reluctantly. As I walked in the door, Maniac leaped from Aunt Jane's arms and disappeared into the house.

Aunt Jane's house was beautiful on the inside and very impressive for a number of reasons. First of all the large spacious living room was full of elegant antique furniture and large paintings mounted in decorative frames that were hung on the walls. There were several china cabinets in the room full of Beleek and Waterford and silver dishes that looked very old and expensive.

In addition, two of the walls in the living room were covered with floor to ceiling book shelves and there must have been several thousand books on display. But my eyes were drawn most to the small framed portraits of cats that were placed all over the room, and the numerous porcelain cats that were in all sizes, sitting on desks, tables and every other available surface in every corner of the room. I was fascinated by one large cat that sat on a table in the corner and I thought he was so realistic that I was convinced that it was looking at me.

Then the cat suddenly moved and I realized that this was not a porcelain cat -- it was Maniac who had picked a strategic spot to keep an eye on me.

Brian moved over to the book cases and I followed him over. As we began to peruse the books, Aunt Jane said she would make a cup of tea and a sandwich for us, but I told her not to bother that I was not hungry. The truth was that I wanted to get out of this place as soon as possible, and the tea would only delay us.

But Aunt Jane waved my objections aside. "Of course you will have tea and sandwich; you are on your lunch hour. You are not leaving here until you have the tea."

So, I knew I was stuck, and I raised no more objections.

"You're afraid of the cat, aren't you?" said Brian. "He frightens you, doesn't he? You wish now you hadn't asked to see him. Look -- he is staring at you. But don't make too much eye contact with him or he will jump on you."

I looked around to see where the cat was and found him sitting on an end table no more than four feet from me, his cold green eyes fixed on me with malice.

"Can't you chase him?" I said to Brian.

"Why don't you chase him?" he said

Of course I wouldn't even try, and I moved closer to Brian and turned to face the cat, because I was afraid to have him behind me.

"Don't stare at him," said Brian "Or you will be sorry."

"I'm not staring at him at all. I just don't want him behind me," I said.

The tense situation was interrupted by the arrival of Aunt Jane from the kitchen, with a large tray full of cups, a plate of sandwiches, and a teapot.

She waved us over to the dining room table and laid out the meal for us. She placed several sandwiches on Brian's plate and two on mine and then went off into the kitchen again.

The sandwiches looked and smelled very good: one was made of ham; the other was made of canned salmon. I was just reaching over to pick up the salmon sandwich when Maniac hopped up on the table and placed a long black furry paw on the salmon sandwich and then glared at me venomously as if defying me to do anything about it. When I did not react, he started to gulp down the sandwich and finished it in a flash. Then he looked me over carefully before polishing off the second sandwich. After that he hopped down to the floor and began to purr.

While this was going on Brian continued to munch on his sandwiches, and the only thing he did was to say in a very low voice -- "You are a very bold cat, Maniac."

Maniac responded by spitting at him and taking a swipe at him with his paw.

Brian did not offer me any of his sandwiches, but left me sitting there at the table speechless, afraid to move and cursing myself for being here in the first place.

Aunt Jane came out of the kitchen a short time later and when she saw the empty plates she said to me that she was glad that I discovered I was hungry after all and had ate up all my sandwiches.

Aunt Jane said she was going to give Maniac a can of sardines, his favorite meal.

"He is very picky about what he eats. Nothing but the best for him. He won't touch ordinary food at all. He will only eat sardines of a certain brand.

"He likes King Oscar brand and no other. I once tried to give him a cheaper brand and he flung the sardines all over the place. It took me a week to get the place clean."

She then went on to say that "his father," had spoiled him when he was a kitten.

While Aunt Jane was taking the dishes into the kitchen, Brian whispered to me:

"She means Mr. McCauley, her friend who brought Maniac here. And she doesn't know Maniac eats out of trash cans and steals dog food from small dogs. King Oscar – that's a joke."

Maniac was looking at him as he spoke and hissed at him when he finished. Then, Aunt Jane arrived back in the dining room.

She seemed to be in a chatty mood and she began to share personal information that people do not usually share` with total strangers. I could not imagine my mother telling someone she just met things that were best left unsaid.

"I suppose Brian has told you all about Old McCauley. Brian is a blabbermouth that tells everybody everything. Old McCauley was a great friend," Aunt Jane said; "He was the only one who really understood Maniac. He had control over Maniac and was very good to him, even though Maniac seemed to like me more than he liked him.

"McCauley wanted to marry me, but I just couldn't put up with that constant drinking. But I miss him anyway and we had some great times together."

I asked her what happened to McCauley, and she told me that when Dipso, the other cat, went missing McCauley went out into the woods and along the river behind the house to look for him. She said he really was very fond of Dipso and he said he would not rest until he found him.

McCauley took Maniac along to help in the search. Maniac came back after an hour, but there was no sign of McCauley. The following morning McCauley was found drowned in the river and it was not known what had happened to him.

"He had scratches on his face when he was found," said Brian, looking over at Maniac.

"The scratches must have come from the bushes along the river bank," said Aunt Jane.

But Brian seemed determined to make a point and he plunged ahead.

"Remember the time the cat kept the plumber from leaving the bathroom for five hours?" said Brian.

Aunt Jane looked at me and gave a nervous laugh. Then she turned to me.

"You must not pay any attention to Brian. He exaggerates and he tries to make out that the cat is off his head. The plumber was mean to him and took a swipe at him when the cat got in his way in the bathroom. So Maniac kept threatening him every time he tried to leave the bathroom. I was out shopping and was not aware of the situation until I came home. But that is normal behavior for a cat, and one should not exaggerate the importance of this."

Brian said it was time to go back to school, so we said goodbye to Aunt Jane and headed out the door, and I for one was very glad that the visit was over.

Although the cat had done nothing to me except steal my sandwiches and give me dirty looks, I definitely got the impression that he did not care for me very much. And I could definitely say for sure that I did not like him very much either. In fact, I thought he was creepy, and the most unusual animal I had ever seen.

On the way back to the school, Brian told me a number of stories about the cat that clearly showed that he was convinced that the cat was indeed a maniac.

He said that when Aunt Jane first got the cat she and McCauley used to go away for several days on holiday, and they would leave plenty of food and milk out for the cat to eat when they were away. But they had to put an end to these holidays because when they came back they would find that Maniac had urinated and defecated all over the house.

This particular tale did not surprise me because we once had a cat that did the same thing. Pets get angry if they are left alone.

After McCauley was found dead, Aunt Jane tried to go off by herself for an overnight stay with friends, but just as she was ready to go out the door, her car keys went missing and she had to stay at home. The following day the keys turned up on the kitchen table.

One time Aunt Jane had ignored Maniac all morning and he got even by locking her out of the house. She had gone out to the garden to get some vegetables without taking her keys with her and when she returned she found the door slammed shut and she was unable to get in.

She went to a next door neighbor and asked him to get a ladder and go in a bedroom window on the second floor, but when the neighbor got up to the window, Maniac was waiting for him and drove him off with howls and scratches.

Eventually the guardi were called and one of them was able to go in the window after spraying Maniac in the face with some sort of spray.

Maniac hated everyone in uniform after that and was even mean to the postman when he came around.

By the time we got back to school I had heard enough about this strange cat, and I couldn't understand why Brian or Aunt Jane did not get rid of this contrary animal. It seemed to me they had two choices: They could continue to live with the problem; or they could solve it by getting rid of Maniac in some way.

I told this to Brian and he said that I just did not understand all aspects of the problem. He said anyone who got on the wrong side of Maniac came to a bad end. McCauley's mother, who tried to have Maniac drowned was killed in a car accident, and McCauley himself, who wanted to try and find Dipso, who Maniac may have murdered, was found in the river. So plotting against Maniac could be a very dangerous thing to do.

At this point I was convinced the cat had driven both Brian and his aunt around the bend, and their obsession with him was very unhealthy.

We parted at the school and I went to my class and he went to his and I did not talk to him for more than a week. When we did meet it was the last day of class before the end of the school year, and we spoke for only a few moments and the cat never came up at all in our conversation and I did not see him again during the long summer holidays.

During the long summer months in Dungloe I found myself thinking about this strange cat quite often, and I even found myself telling other people about him. At one point the thought occurred to me that I was becoming like Brian Curran, which gave me the shudders.

When I returned to school in September several weeks passed before I became aware that I had not seen Brian around, so I asked about him and was told his aunt had died suddenly during the summer.

I immediately had a ridiculous thought – Maniac had killed her; but I banished this thought quickly because I knew this was the way Brian Curran thought. Later in the day I found out that Brian and his mother had inherited the house and were busy moving in. Because of this, his mother decided to keep Brian home from school for several weeks to help with the move.

When I heard that I wondered about Maniac again. Surely Brian and his mother would not be foolish enough to move in with this crazy animal? Surely not.

Although I was not a close friend of Brian I did know him well enough to feel I had a duty to go to his house and sympathize with him about his aunt's death.

Attendance at a wake is a very serious social obligation in Donegal. If a person does not attend a wake it sends a message to the bereaved family that the person who does not attend feels no obligation to sympathize with them.

If you are out of the area when the death occurred or did not hear of the death because you lived in a different area some contact with the bereaved family was required later.

Brian had lived on the outskirts of Letterkenny and only attended St.Eunan's in the daytime; my home was thirty miles away in Dungloe and I boarded with a family in Letterkenny while going to school. So, during the summer I had no contact with him and was not aware of Jane's death.

But I was more than a little nervous about going down to Aunt Jane's old home because of the possibility of seeing Maniac again. During the summer, I had several nightmares about Maniac stalking me and then ambushing me, and even though I knew that it was ridiculous to be afraid of the cat, I could not get rid of the paranoia about him nevertheless.

I waited until the school day was completed before I reluctantly walked down the street towards Aunt Jane's house. As I approached the house the curtains on one of the front windows parted and a spooky black face with cold green eyes looked out. I got the creeps: the cat was still around. I wondered if Maniac knew I was coming and was welcoming me.

I almost turned away there and then, but pride got the better of me because I thought it would be ridiculous to let a cat chase me away from the house. So I soldiered on up to the door and rang the bell.

Brian and the cat met me at the door. Brian looked very depressed. He was on edge. I expressed my condolences about Aunt Jane and Brian accepted them politely. I could not take my eyes off the cat, which had undergone a dramatic change. Gone was the immaculately groomed fur and the arrogant stare; the cat now looked dirty and bedraggled, and the arrogance in his eyes was replaced by a seething rage.

The bold bad cat now seemed like a psycho cat. I thought it wise to get out of there as soon as possible, so I turned away from Brian telling him I would see him at school. But Brian was having none of that: "You must come in and talk to my mother. She would think it terrible if you went away without seeing her."

So I went into the living room with Brian in the lead and the cat walking silently at my heels.

I had never met Brian's mother before and I was amazed at how much she looked like Aunt Jane. Brian must have seen my expression and he offered an explanation:

"Mom and Aunt Jane were twins – identical twins. Just like Dipso and Maniac."

I offered my condolences to Brian's mother, and then I made a mistake: I asked her what the cause of Aunt Jane's death. She seemed very hurt by the question, and turned away from me.

It was Brian who responded, and he responded by asking another question:

"What did you hear about her death?"

I said all I heard was that she was found dead. I had no details, and I did not really need details.

Brian changed the subject by asking his mother to go and make tea for the guest. I was about to tell them I did not want any, but I remembered that would be very bad manners, so I sat on the couch quietly, keeping an eye on Maniac.

Maniac seemed preoccupied with something and only rarely looked in my direction. He seemed to be staring up the stairs at the balcony on the top of the stairs as if there was something up there.

"He won't let us clean him or take him out for a walk," said Brian.

"Aunt Jane used to take him down to the park every day so he could ambush and kill sparrows and starlings. But he won't go anymore, and he doesn't even bother with the birds that sometimes land in the back garden."

Brian's mother came back with the tea and sandwiches and laid them out on the table. I watched Maniac to see if he was going to steal my sandwiches again, but he paid no attention to me and continued to stare up at the balcony. Suddenly he stood up.

"Watch what happens next," Brian said.

I stared at the cat. Slowly the cat walked up the stairs to the balcony and walked across the landing to a closed door at the other end, mewing as he strode across the floor.

"That door leads to the bedroom that Aunt Jane slept in," said Brian. "He used to sleep up there every night with her and he still sleeps there. We tried to take her stuff out of there but he won't let us. He has made it very clear that he wants everything to be left in place."

As I listened to Brian my reaction to him was the same as it had been months previously when I first met the cat in this house: I thought that the Currans were a little off for tolerating this situation. I believed that they were more to blame for the situation than this psychotic cat.

If we had a cat like this in our house my father would have dumped him in the river, or got Terry, our Alsatian dog, to put manners on him. They certainly would not have let this cat institute a reign of terror, and would have solved the problem promptly.

Of course I knew many people whose behavior was a little bizarre when it came to their relationship with their pets, so the Currans were not that unusual. I had a relative who was nutty about her two dogs and every Christmas she used to send Christmas cards from the dogs to our family. We knew another family who went deeply in debt to pay for an operation to save their dog's life. And we knew yet another family who spent their life savings on an operation for their pet goat.

But the actions of all of those families were based on a deep love for their pets, which was also returned by those pets, and this was very different from the relationship between the Currans and Maniac. In this instance fear and intimidation seemed to be the basis for the relationship, and this made it so perverse. Who in their right mind would let a small animal like that gain control of the house?

Maniac stood in front of the bedroom door for a few moments and then he began to wriggle his body and dig his claws into the carpet as if someone was tickling him and petting him. Then the bedroom door clicked open and Maniac slipped into the room and the door closed behind him.

I was mesmerized by the scene on the balcony. "How did he get the door open?" I asked.

"We do not know, " said Brian.

"He spends a great deal of time up there since Jane died," said Brian's mother. "Somehow I don't think he believes she is dead. He acts like she is still around. Maybe he blames himself for her death, because she accidentally took that overdose after he ran away for a week."

"What overdose?" I had not heard about an overdose.

"She yelled at him one day when he wouldn't let a plumber into the house, and he ran out the door and vanished. It was the first time she had yelled at him and the first time he had ever run away. I think he was punishing her, "said Brian.

"She was in an awful state for a week," said Brian's mother. "She cried all the time and searched the whole town for him. She even offered a big reward to anyone who would find him. And all that time he was hiding up the tree outside the sitting room window, hidden by leaves and peeking in at her. Mrs. Johnson across the street saw him and wondered what he was doing up the tree."

Maniac's mind games led directly to Jane's death.

"She always took sleeping pills but one night she took too many." said Brian.

He then went on to tell me that the body was discovered after the cat began to screech and howl at the front door, as if he knew what had happened and was raising the alarm.

I decided it was time to go. I had heard more than I needed to know about the Currans and their cat. And I decided I would never ask about this cat again. I had enough. At this point I got up to leave and while I was saying goodbye the door upstairs clicked open and Maniac came down the stairs slowly, as if he was following someone. He went into the kitchen and began to mew and moan and scratch the floor as if someone was petting him. I knew it was time to leave.

Then Brian's mother dropped a bombshell – very casually. "We are not going to live here after all. We have decided against it. We are going to sell the house and move back to our old house. We are not taking the cat with us," she said. "Would you want this nice cat. He is a full-bred Persian. He is very valuable."

I thanked her very much but said I could not take the cat. My father did not like cats. My mother did not like cats. And Terry our dog did not like cats either. I did not tell her that I did not like this particular cat, and if the truth were told I would rather spend a night in a jail cell with a lunatic that spend a night in a house with Maniac.

I took my leave and hoped never to lay eyes on this cat ever again.

Several weeks later, I was surprised to see Brian back at school looking very relaxed and very healthy. The brooding Brian seemed to have gone off on a holiday.

I wondered if some way had been found to create a final solution to the Maniac problem, but I did not ask him and I hoped he would volunteer the information because I was curious. He did.

"We have sold Aunt Jane's house and moved back to our own house," He said. "I am very happy about it."

He must have seen the big question in my eyes so he said: "The new owners are from Belfast. They love cats and were happy to take him."

"And how about Maniac?" Is he happy with them?"

"I don't know," said Brian. "And I don't want to know. I have never gone back there and they haven't called us."

And that was the last I ever heard of Maniac.

But sometimes, in the years that followed, I would think of him and wish I were a fly on the wall in Aunt Jane's old home to see what is going on inside. However that was as far as my curiosity took me. I would never have dreamed of knocking on the door and asking the new owners for an update on the cat.

That would be asking for trouble.

*   *   *

THE HANDPRINT ON THE WALL

The former Carbon County Jail, in Jim Thorpe, Pennsylvania, is in the heart of the historic anthracite coal-mining region, and is one of the town's major tourist attractions. Thousands pass through the jail's grim corridors every year viewing the cells that housed convicted criminals for more than a hundred years and hearing lectures from the guides about the jail's most famous prisoners: the Molly Maguires who were imprisoned and executed here in the 1870s.

One cell in the cellblock on the first floor merits special attention from the guides – the cell with a handprint on the wall, which according to the legend, was made by Molly Maguire leader Alec Campbell on June 21, 1877, as he left the cell to meet the hangman. According to the legend, Campbell placed his hand on the wall and swore to his innocence, and the handprint has remained there ever since.

Alec Campbell was my great uncle.

I first heard about Alec Campbell from my father back in Dungloe, County Donegal, in the 1940s. My father used to tell customers in the family bar all about his Uncle Alec, who, according to my father, was framed by the Pinkerton Detective Agency on instructions from Franklin Gowen and other Pennsylvania coal mining barons, and sent to the gallows for a crime he did not commit.

Campbell was one of more than twenty members of the Ancient Order of Hibernians who were executed in Pennsylvania during this period. The prosecution claimed that these AOH members belonged to the Molly Maguires, a secret terrorist group within the AOH, who, it was alleged, were responsible for a dozen murders in the 1870s.

My father was very passionate about Alec's innocence and equally passionate that Gowen and the Pinkertons were guilty of his murder.

After I arrived out in the United States in 1957 I learned that there were two versions of the Alec Campbell story in circulation, each at odds with the other.

One version claimed that Alec Campbell and the rest of the Molly Maguires were trade union activists who were the victims of a capitalist conspiracy to destroy the Workers Benevolent Association, the miners union. The WBA had fought Franklin Gowen, Charles Parrish, Asa Packer and other mine owners for higher wages and better working conditions for mineworkers and the union had become so troublesome to the mine barons that they hatched a conspiracy to get rid of them. This conspiracy involved the hiring of the Pinkerton Detective Agency to assassinate mine supervisors and then to blame the AOH for the murders.

The second version of the Molly saga current in the mining regions characterized the Molly Maguires as a group of murderous thugs who terrorized the coal mining regions for almost a decade, and that Alec Campbell was one of the leaders of the organization.

Both versions were and are still subscribed to today with a great deal of passion by different segments of the population in Carbon, Luzerne, Schuykill, and Northumberland counties in Pennsylvania.

The different interpretations of the Molly saga are illustrated by the debates that continue on some of the Molly Maguire boards on the Internet at the present time. This debate is heated and both sides adhere passionately to their version of history.

The anti-Molly faction produce a steady stream of invective against the long-dead Molly leaders accusing them of mass murder and all types of heinous crimes; the pro-Molly lobby are passionate about the innocence of the Mollies and are working to get a resolution passed by the Pennsylvania Legislature calling for the guilty verdicts to be set aside.

The pro-Mollie faction believe that the Mollies were denied due process in the courts in the 1870s and were in fact "lynched" by the courts, which had become a servant of coal company interests.

A mock trial of Alec Campbell was held in the Carbon County Courthouse in 1993, presided over by Judge John Lavelle of Carbon County.

The testimony at the trial was based on the original trial testimony in 1876, and a jury was selected to hear the case. Alec Campbell was found innocent this time around.

Two years later another mock trial was held in the county courthouse in Pottsville, based on the trial of Jack Kehoe, another alleged Molly Maguire leader, with the same results: Kehoe was found innocent.

Many of the anti-Molly individuals on the internet are descendants of Pinkerton detectives, or descendants of informers in the pay of the mine owners.

One prominent apologist for Franklin Gowen and the Pinkertons is a prominent Columbus, Ohio, lawyer, who is a descendant of Irish-born James McParland, the Pinkerton bounty hunter, who sent many fellow Irishmen, including Alec Campbell, to the gallows by providing false testimony at their trials. This lawyer hides behind a screen name on the internet and does not admit a relationship with McParland.

Other anti-Mollie activists are comprised of those who do not have a great deal of affection for Irish Catholics.

Those who champion the Mollies are descendants of the Molly Maguires; supporters of organized labor; or people who despise the bounty hunting activities of the Pinkertons during this period of American history.

The handprint on the cell wall has been the target of a great deal of curiosity for more than a hundred years.

Because of the handprint, the Carbon County Jail at Mauch Chunk{Jim Thorpe} was a tourist attraction as far back as the 1880s. The name Mauch Chunk was the original Native-American name of the town, but in the 1950s, the name was changed to Jim Thorpe in honor of the great American athlete, who had a mix of Irish and Native-American heritage.

My father arrived in the United States as an immigrant in the late 1890s, and eventually settled in Bayonne, New Jersey, where he had cousins already established.

After he found a job with Standard Oil and settled down to his new life in America, he headed out one weekend to Mauch Chunk to see for himself the handprint that had been so much part of his family folklore back in Ireland for the previous twenty years. He found the jail, which was being used as an active prison at the time, was also tourist attraction, which drew crowds every weekend to see Alec Campbell's handprint on the wall. The day my father arrived more than a hundred tourists were present during his visit. All seemed to be in a very festive mood.

In contrast, my father's visit to the jail was an emotional experience for him.

In the years that followed, my father would talk about how the hand's imprint had deeply moved him. He felt his visit provided him with a religious experience. However, he disliked the carnival atmosphere created by the tourists who were peering into the cell and making all kinds of comments about the handprint and about the man who left it there before he mounted the gallows.

My father had never known Alec Campbell personally because Alec had left Ireland before my father was born, but he was well aware of the effect of the execution on his relatives. My father's father, Neil Campbell, talked frequently about the great injustice of his brother's execution, and Alec's mother, Mary, who lived on until 1908, always claimed her son was murdered by Franklin Gowen and the Pinkertons.

Other members of the family had suffered as a result of the execution and were branded all their life as the descendants of a vicious criminal, a charge that upset them to no end since they believed in his innocence.

So, my father's trip to Mauch Chunk was something of a pilgrimage to a place where a terrible family tragedy had unfolded twenty years previously.

After visiting the jail he went up to nearby Summit Hill to the cemetery at St Joseph's Church, where Alec Campbell and several other executed Molly Maguires had been buried, and he said a prayer at Alec's grave. Then he left the Mauch Chunk area and never returned again.

However, the visit had made a tremendous impression on him, and even when he returned to Donegal in the 1920s with a wife and three young daughters to open a hotel and restaurant there, he talked about Alec Campbell and the Molly Maguires for the rest of his life.

The Alec Campbell handprint continued as a tourist attraction until the 1930s when the sheriff in charge of the jail at that time, who was out of patience with the hordes of tourists arriving at his facility every week, took a number of steps to try to put an end to the circus.

The first step was to close the jail to tourists. By doing this he hoped that interest in the handprint would gradually die down. His next step was to declare that Alec Campbell had never been in that cell at all – that it was another condemned Molly Maguire named Thomas Fischer who had left that particular cell on the morning of his execution. The sheriff did not say that the handprint belonged to Fischer; he was only determined to eliminate Campbell's connection with the handprint. It did not work, because the handprint continued to be linked with Campbell in the decades that followed.

My brother Bernie made a pilgrimage to Mauch Chunk in 1942 during World War 11 and was able to talk his way into the jail to get a look at the famous handprint.

Bernie was able to get in because he was in the dress uniform of an officer in the United States Merchant Marine, and because of this the sheriff who was running the jail was happy to let him in. Bernie, like my father, was deeply moved by the experience, and for the rest of his life he talked about Alec Campbell and the way he met his end.

My wife Eileen and I visited the jail for the first time in 1975, and we were allowed in to see the cell and the famous handprint when I identified myself as a relative of Alec Campbell. We had our photograph taken in the cell with the handprint in the background.

The jail was still an active prison at this time and it was a very strange experience for us to walk through the central courtyard towards the Alec Campbell cell, while prisoners crowded around us curious about what we were doing in their domain. I suppose the prisoners in this county jail were not of a violent nature because otherwise the sheriff would not have allowed us among them, but it was still a very unusual experience.

When I saw the handprint I was very curious about it and I reached up and placed my hand in the outline of the handprint. It was a perfect fit. I don't recall having any emotional reaction to the handprint, but I disliked the small cramped cell and the covered courtyard, which looked like a mini Alcatraz. It thought it a place that was extremely depressing.

The sheriff pointed to the end if the courtyard and he told us that the gallows had been erected there, and that Alec and three other Mollies had been hanged there at 10AM on June 21, 1877. He said admission tickets were very much in demand to see the hanging and a huge crowd was admitted to witness the event. The sheriff said that only a fraction of those who wanted to be present was admitted because there just was not room in the courtyard and the balcony.

"They built the gallows outside the cells where Campbell and the others were being held, and when they were finished they tested the gallows by dropping bags of sand tied to the end of a rope," the sheriff said.

"The tests were repeated time and time again and it must have been very hard on the condemned men who had to listen to all the noise. But the sheriff conducting the executions was indifferent to their feelings."

"The condemned prisoners had to watch all that, and so had their relatives who came to visit them. The night before the executions a group of school children led by a Presbyterian Minister staged a square dance on the platform of the gallows. A lot of very strange things happened here during that time"

Although I had not become emotionally involved with the jail or the handprint, the visit did inspire me to write a book about the Alec Campbell case, *A Molly Maguire Story,* which was published in 1992.

During my research for *A Molly Maguire Story,* I focused briefly in on the issue of the handprint on the wall to see if there was any reference to it in the days and weeks immediately after the execution, but found only one reference in a story published in the *New York Times* the day before Campbell's execution. In his interview with the *Times* reporter Campbell said he would prove his innocence in the last hour of his life, but was not specific about how he would achieve this. Legend has it he placed his hand on the cell wall as he was being led out to die, and the "proof of innocence" is thought to be the presence of the hand on the wall.

There are those who accept the handprint on the wall as a genuine supernatural phenomenon, and there are those who dismiss it as either a hoax or a phenomenon that must have some scientific explanation.

Those who believe the handprint is supernatural in origin accept its presence without question. They also believe that Alec Campbell is innocent and that the handprint is proof of this innocence; they have no doubts at all about this. However, these believers can offer no proof to support their convictions, and at the end of the day, their convictions are based on faith and faith alone.

Those who believe that the handprint is a hoax that has been perpetrated for many decades by the staff at the jail have no proof to offer either, and even the most casual examination of this argument reveals some basic weaknesses in this theory.

If this theory were correct it would mean that the sheriff and his staff who were in charge of the jail back in the 1890s had conspired to hoodwink my father into believing that this was his uncle's handprint on the wall.

It would mean that the sheriff and his staff who ran the jail in the 1940s had conspired to get my brother to believe that the handprint belonged to his great uncle; and it would mean that the sheriff and his staff who operated the jail in 1975 were playing games with me when I visited the jail. Not only that it would mean that every sheriff and all the staff from the 1877 onwards to the time that the jail closed down were all in on the plot and not one of them ever broke their silence and talked about it.

That theory seems far too incredible to entertain, because the odds of such a thing happening would be off the scale. So, I am inclined to dismiss this theory.

The possibility of some scientific theory that would explain the handprint is equally problematic. Some belief that at some point in time shortly after the execution of Alec Campbell a worker or a prisoner who was in the cell placed a dirty hand on the wall and that there was some chemicals on this person's hand that soaked into the cement plaster on the wall and the handprint has remained on the wall ever since.

The problem with this theory is that over the years the legend not only attributes the handprint to Alec Campbell, the legend also states that numerous attempts were made over the years to paint over the handprint.

On several occasions, according to the folklore, the plaster was chipped down to the basic stonework, and then plastered again, and the handprint always reemerged.

Tom and Betty Lou McBride, current owners of the jail who operate it as a landmark tourist attraction, have in their files a testimony from a contractor who worked in the cell thirty five years ago removing the plaster down to the stone wall. He states that when the wall was plastered again the hand reemerged.

A local parish priest in Jim Thorpe has provided an affidavit that states that when he was a teenager the resident parish priest at the time had him paint three coats of paint over the hand, and then the cell door was padlocked overnight. He states the handprint was back in the morning.

So, the theory of one dirty handprint sitting on the wall undisturbed for 130 years is as shaky as the theory that it is all a hoax cooked up by successive sheriffs. It is just too far fetched to be credible

So, what then is the explanation for the handprint?

Frankly, I do not know, but I believe that in the final analysis, there could be some other explanation for the handprint that does not extend the bounds of credibility, or is not based on faith alone. However, if such an explanation exists, I have yet to come across it.

As for myself. I have not come to any conclusion one way or the other about the handprint. I take the same approach to this particular phenomenon that I do to reports about the existence of UFOs. I believe that there are life forms out there in space because I find it incredible that humankind would be alone in the universe.

But unless I meet up with a UFO myself I suspend any judgment on what other people claim to have seen. In the same way, I also suspend judgment on whether or not the handprint on the cell wall in Jim Thorpe is the product of a supernatural incident, and I continue to keep an open mind on the subject.

One of the reasons for my unwillingness to respond one way or another to the legend has to do with my natural skepticism about such phenomenon. My instincts are to question something like this.

I have been in the cell many times in recent years and I can honestly say that I found nothing supernatural about the atmosphere in the cell, or in any other part of the jail I visited, including the dungeon.

This of course does not mean there was nothing there to sense, it just means that I do not sense it. My inability to sense any indication of the family tragedy that happened in this place is not proof that the handprint was not genuine – it just means I did not get the emotional reaction my father and brother had experienced -- which proves nothing.

Meanwhile, thousands of visitors stream through the facility, some relatives of the Molly Maguires, others who just want to visit the famous jail.

The busses roll up to the door carry visitors from all over the world who want to tour the jail and see the famous handprint on the wall.

Almost 200,000 people have visited the jail, since it was opened to the public. These visitors have come from all fifty states and thirty foreign countries, including Ireland.

Tom and Betty Lou McBride own and operate the jail, and in the last 12 years they have interviewed many of these visitors and noted their reaction to the jail in general and the handprint in particular. Since the jail has the reputation of being haunted by a number of ghosts, including the ghost of Alec Campbell, the McBrides have compiled a huge file of testimony gathered from those visitors who claim they have sensed the supernatural while visiting the jail. Betty Lou McBride published a book in 2005 that   includes the testimony of many of these visitors.

The following are examples of the type of stories that are included in the book: On two separate occasions five years apart, two young girls, from different parts of the country, claim to have seen a man in the locked Alec Campbell cell, who stared out at them. But their parents saw nothing, even while the children insisted that the man was staring at them.

The McBrides will not allow any flash photography focused on the handprint because they have been told that excessive flashes might damage the handprint, but some visitors try to photograph the inside of the cell anyway with some unusual results. Tom Bride said he personally witnessed the fact that flash bulbs on cameras would not work when visitors pointed their cameras through the door of the cell.

However, the flashes would work if the visitor moved away from the cell. He has no explanation for this, but he said it occurs frequently.

Scores of visitors have had mild panic attacks in various parts of the jail, while others have claimed to sense an unseen "presence" near the Alec Campbell cell, or near where the gallows was located.

Of course, not every visitor comes across the resident ghosts in the jail, and the majority of visitors do not sense anything supernatural at all anywhere in the jail.

I visit the Old Jail at least once a year to attend an annual Mass organized by the Alec Campbell Division of the Ancient Order of Hibernians in Jim Thorpe, on the anniversary of the Molly Maguire executions.

An altar is erected where the gallows once stood and descendants of the executed Mollies attend to keep their memory alive.

The priest who says the Mass always gives a sermon about the legal lynching that took place in the Jail on June 21, 1877, a day that has been named "The Day of the Rope".

During my attendance at the Mass, I say a prayer for the soul of Alec Campbell, Edward Kelly, Hugh Doyle, and Jack Donahue, who died so violently in this place on that day.

Then all the attendees go down the street to the Molly Maguire Pub and Restaurant to have lunch and raise a toast to the memory of the Mollies.

The Old Jail Museum opens at 12pm for tours Memorial Day through October. It is located on Broadway, above the Opera House.

Jim Thorpe is located in northeast Pennsylvania and the town has numerous other attractions in addition to the Old Jail.

THE OLD JAIL, JIM THORPE

ALEC CAMPBELL

A DEATH IN THE FAMILY

The death of a child is the worst experience that can happen to any parent, and when the child dies suddenly and violently the experience is all the more devastating. It is an event that no parent completely recovers from. Much has been written about "closure" and "healing" in connection with the aftermath of such an event, but for many, if not for most parents, there is no closure, and there is only limited healing. At best there is only the learned ability to endure the pain and to hope that time will make it more bearable.

My wife Eileen and I lost our thirteen year old son Padraic on December 5, 1985, and hardly a day goes by since then that we do not think of him. He was killed by a drunken driver who fled the scene and left him to die at the side of the road.

We were devastated by the event and completely unprepared on how to cope with it.

Our relatives and friends were also devastated and most of them had no idea how to console us. Their efforts at comforting us not only did not make us feel better, it only made us feel more depressed.

One close friend came to me the day after Padraic was killed and gave me some advice on how I should cope with the disaster: he said I should focus on the thirteen good years I had with my son and not focus on the abrupt ending of his life. He believed I would accept the reality of what happened if I would convince myself that this was Padraic's allotted time on this world and I had been given the gift of his company for that length of time.

I suppose this man thought this was a very sensible approach to the tragedy and I am sure he thought it made a great deal of sense to him.

But as I looked at him I wondered if he would take the same approach if he lost one of his own children, and somehow I thought he would not. Indeed I knew he would have been as devastated as I was, and if anyone had given him the advice he had just given me he would have thought that that person was extremely insensitive.

The reality was that any enjoyment I might have had at the thirteen years of Padraic's life was buried in the pain of the knowledge that I would never enjoy a moment of his company again.

A priest who came to visit us was just as insensitive as my friend, and I thought at the time that he should have known better how to comfort a grieving parent.

The priest's approach was to tell us that he was convinced that Padraic was now in Heaven, and that we should not mourn him but celebrate the fact that he was now up there with God. He said God must have wanted him and therefore he came and got him, and that it was a great honor to have been chosen by God.

As I listened to him I thought that only a bachelor who had never loved a child, or been loved by a child, would think that such an argument would make any sense to grieving parents.

The irony of this approach was that while it was designed to draw Eileen and me closer to God, it had the opposite effect on me because I thought God had no right to take our child and break our hearts in the process. His little sermon was the type of approach that drove parents away from God: it did not bring them closer to Him.

My brother James had an idea of how to comfort us, but his approach was no more sensible than the rest of the advice we received.

James thought we should consider adopting a son to replace Padraic, and I was very blunt in my response to James: I told we had not lost a pet dog that could be replaced by a pup. I said Padraic was unique and as such was irreplaceable. After that James did not bring the subject up again.

None of the people who gave this advice intended to do us any harm. They did not know how to console us and they offered the advice that seemed sensible to them, not knowing they were only making matters worse. Losing a child is a unique experience and only those who have lost children know how to console another grieving parent.

The ideal approach to a grieving parent is very simple: be a very good listener, because the parents feel compelled to talk about their loss and vent the agony that is overwhelming them. Only give advice if you are a bereaved parent yourself and have been down that road and know what to say.... and what not to say.

Padraic had been killed using a brand new skateboard that I had bought him. He had only been using the skateboard for a few days when he was struck by a speeding car while crossing the street.

Eileen did not like skateboards because she thought they were dangerous, but many of Padraic's friends had skateboards and I saw no harm in getting him a brand new one which I thought were far less dangerous than the old skateboards he sometimes borrowed from his friends. His death on the skateboard added an element of guilt to my grief, because I thought that if I had not bought him the skateboard he would still be alive.

PADRAIC

I found some comfort from the fact that nobody else seemed to blame me for my son's death. More than one person told me that I was only trying to be good to my son by buying him the skateboard, not trying to kill him, but the feelings of guilt were very difficult to shake especially since Eileen had been so opposed to skateboards in the first place.

I went through a period when I could not bare to watch a child using a skateboard, and when I did see one I had to resist the temptation to approach their parents and tell them how dangerous they were.

But ultimately I came to the conclusion that it was not the skateboards that were dangerous, it was the manner in which they are used, and this could make the difference between life and death.

In Padraic's case he had crossed a two lane highway to a nearby shopping center and he did not have the green light to make the crossing.

There was a car approaching on the inside lane towards him traveling within the 35-mile per hour speed limit, and he apparently thought he had plenty of time to get across, because the car was hundreds of yards down the road.

But Padraic did not see a second car traveling on the outside lane doing sixty miles an hour, because the first car hid it from Padraic's view, and when Padraic was out in the middle of the road the car ploughed into him, tossing him like a rag doll onto the side of the road and breaking almost every bone in his body.

The car's windshield was broken and the driver got out briefly and looked at Padraic's body, then he got into his car and sped away.

The driver might have got away completely with this crime were it not for the fact that another driver jotted down his license plate and he was arrested in New York City the following morning. The car with the broken windshield was in the driveway, and when the police went into the man's apartment they found a book of Yellow Pages on the kitchen table open at the section for windshields.

Obviously he had no intention of taking responsibility for my son's death.

The police did an investigation of the driver who turned out to be a 22-year-old Greek national who had over-stayed his visa, and he was driving a car with no insurance and no registration.

It could not be determined who owned the car, but later it turned out he was working for a Greek company that exported used American cars abroad, and this car could have been one of them, but prior ownership could not be determined because the identification numbers had been filed down.

The driver said he had bought the car for $10,000 cash from another Greek who had left the country, but he could not produce receipts. His employer said he knew nothing about the car.

We got a call from a neighbor that the driver had been in a neighborhood bar for several hours before the accident and when I checked with the bartender he told me that the Greek was a regular and had numerous whiskeys there that night before he drove away.

I told this to the police, but they told me that this could not be used as evidence against him because he had fled the scene and there was no way to prove he had been drunk behind the wheel.

The police said it would be pointless to give him a blood test the following day because he could say he had a number of drinks after the accident to calm his nerves.

The police had charged him with vehicular homicide after his arrest, which could have got the driver ten years in jail, but the District Attorney's office lowered the charges to leaving the scene of an accident, because the attorney believed he did not have enough witnesses to get a conviction. Leaving the scene of an accident merited only thirty days in jail at that time in New Jersey, even when there was a fatality involved. The laws have changed since then.

The two-day wake at a funeral parlor in Bayonne, NJ, was very difficult to endure. Eileen and I had a wide circle of friends and all of them showed up for the wake.

I had numerous friends and acquaintances from my association with my work at the World Trade Center and the Irish Echo Newspaper and this drew large volumes of people to the funeral home. Eileen was a real estate agent and had a wide circle of friends and business acquaintances and they all showed up. Nora's class at school came to sympathize, and all of Padraic's friends from school and the boy scouts turned up in force.

Then the very fact that a child had died violently attracted people to sympathize with us who might not have turned up if Padraic had been an adult.

In all, lines of people came to pay their respects for two days and it was very hard to keep our composure when we were confronted by so many people, many of whom greeted us while in a very emotional state.

The only time I nearly lost my composure was when an old friend named Charles Comer showed up with Paddy Maloney, leader of the Chieftains, the Irish traditional group. I had written many reviews of Chieftains concerts in the *Irish Echo,* and when Comer, who was Maloney's press agent, told Paddy about what had happened he said he wanted to attend the wake and sympathize with me.

But when Comer told me Maloney had brought his flute along and wanted to play some Irish melodies in Padraic's honor I almost broke down and I told Comer I just did not want him to do that – that I had brought Padraic to a dozen Chieftains' concerts and that listening to Maloney play in the funeral parlor would bring back a flood of memories and I just could not endure it. So, Maloney did not play.

I do not know what Comer told Maloney but I hoped he told him I appreciated the gesture, even if I could not accept the gift of his music. Maloney's heart was in the right place and I know he thought he was making a gesture that would be welcomed by me.

There was a few other incidents at the wake that were unsettling, but they did not have the potential impact that the possibility of hearing Paddy Maloney's flute had.

On the second evening of the wake a police lieutenant in the Jersey City Police Department came to me and told me that the man arrested and charged with vehicular homicide had been released from jail on low bail and the charges against him reduced to leaving the scene of an accident because there were no witnesses against him. He said he was distressed by this but it was the District Attorney's call and the police could do nothing about it. I made no response to him because I could not focus on anything at that moment.

But later I would think it obscene that an illegal alien who had killed a child while driving intoxicated in a car that had no insurance or registration could be released on such low bail and walk away a free man.

Later, a woman came up to me and handed me her card: she said she was a psychiatrist and had been at the scene of the accident and that I would need therapy. She asked me if I wanted to make an appointment, but I just turned on my heel and walked away. I had heard of ambulance chasers but this was the first time I had ever heard of a psychiatrist drumming up business in a funeral parlor. I thought it despicable.

Towards the end of the evening a pompous little man in an ill fitting suit walked past all those waiting in line to sympathize with us and presented himself to Eileen and I. He said he came to represent a member of the Jersey City Council who represented our district and to offer the councilman's sympathy to us.

I was speechless. Several questions came to mind but I did not ask them. Questions such as – why hadn't the councilman come himself?; why did he send a pompous little person like this who thought he was on a very important mission; and why did the councilman not have the common sense to know that in a situation like this sympathies should only be expressed in person. But I said nothing and the little man strutted off--mission accomplished.

I appreciated all the outpouring of sympathy and it provided a temporary buffer for Eileen and me against dwelling on the terrible reality that we had lost our son, even if it lasted for only a few hours at the wake.

As long as we were surrounded by people we were shielded from thinking about the child who lay silently in the open coffin.

But we also knew that all those people who reached out to us would go back to their homes and we would be left alone with the pain of our loss and with no way to lessen it. All we could hope for was that time would give us some relief.

I attended the trial of the Greek immigrant, Christdoulou, who killed my son and for the first time looked into the eyes of the last person to see my son alive before he ploughed into him with his car.

He was a stocky man with a bloated drinker's face and he was very nervous as he walked into the courtroom accompanied by his lawyer. His lawyer approached the judge and told him his client was pleading guilty to leaving the scene of the accident. There would not have been any point in the lawyer doing anything else. The death car was found in Christodoulou's driveway; pieces of the car left at the scene of the accident matched Christodoulou's car; and the Greek had not said anyone else was driving the car. So he could hardly have pleaded anything else.

His lawyer's strategy then was to try and get his client a suspended sentence or a fine, instead of the maximum thirty days that the New Jersey law called for at the time. So, he made a passionate plea to the judge not to jail the man because he was the son of a Greek general and he had come from an excellent family. The lawyer said he had never been in trouble before and he was devastated at the death of the teenager, and that he would give his own life if he could bring the child back again.

So, the lawyer argued for a fine or community service and asked the judge not to put this young man in jail with criminals, because he was not a criminal.

As I listened to the lawyer I doubted very much that his client was in any way sorry for the way his drinking and his speeding had killed my son and ruined our lives, because neither he nor any member of his family had offered any sympathy to us or made any effort to take responsibility for what he had done.

The prosecutor argued for a jail sentence by saying that Christodoulou's conduct was inexcusable: he had run into a child and then left him dying on the side of the road.

The prosecutor made no mention of the drunken driving because he could not prove it. He made no mention of the speeding because he had no witnesses to support this claim. He did not mention that there was no evidence to show who owned the car; no insurance on the car; false license plates on the car; and that Christodoulou had no drivers license and he had overstayed his visa and was in effect an illegal alien. He did not mention any of these things because, he said later, they were irrelevant to the charge of leaving the scene of an accident.

The judge listened to both sides and then gave Christodoulou the thirty days in jail, but then watered down the sentence to make it almost meaningless. The defense lawyer asked that his client be allowed to serve the sentence at weekends, because he was attending college and he did not want to interrupt his studies.

The judge went along with this and allowed him to begin his weekend sentence on a Saturday morning and end it on Sunday evening, getting credit for two days in jail while spending only one night there.

Then, there was an allowance for good behavior which chopped off four weekends from the sentence, and four more weekends taken off as a suspended sentence.

Thus, out of the fifteen weekends supposed to have been served, only seven were served and this amounted to seven nights in jail on a thirty-day sentence.

I do not know what exactly the judge was thinking off when he handed out a sentence that could have got the prisoner 10 years in jail if he were sentenced under new laws enacted two years later.

No doubt the prosecutor had a great deal to do with it because he told me before the sentencing that my son had crossed without having a green light and this behavior contributed to the accident. He also said that he could understand the panic that would lead the driver of the car to flee the scene of the accident.

While it is true that Padraic made an unwise choice to skate across the road, he would not have been killed if Christodoulou was not speeding or if his reflexes had not been impaired by alcohol, and the prosecutor's "understanding" of the drunken driver was hard to accept.

When I brought this up with him he was annoyed, and he said that he was at that particular time prosecuting a case where a man walked into a bar and shot another man in the back and killed him.

"You can't compare that crime to your situation. The driver did not mean to kill your son; the other man meant to kill his victim. There is a world of difference."

I told him I disagreed with him. Both crimes led to deaths. My son was as dead as if he had been shot.

I also pointed out that anyone who gets into a car while drunk has a weapon under his control that is as deadly as a pistol. The prosecutor was not interested in discussing other aspects of the case: the possibility that the car was stolen; the lack of insurance or registration; the suggestion by some members of the police that the driver was part of a ring who smuggled stolen cars out of the United States; or the fact the driver was in the country illegally.

As far as the prosecutor was concerned the whole case could be summarized as a case of a teenager skating against the light, and all else was irrelevant.

I tried to get the FBI and Immigration involved but they ignored me because they were all busy chasing dope dealers. I tried to sue the man but he ignored my lawyers and refused to come into court, and my lawyers wouldn't pursue the case because there was no one with assets to sue. The car was an orphan. There was no insurance company. Christodoulou said he was a penniless student. So the case died, and we had to live with our grief.

I stayed out of work for two weeks after Padraic was killed and spent the time going from one amusement park to another in Florida. This activity was designed to keep eight-year-old Nora's mind off the loss of her brother and to keep us from sitting at home brooding. But even though the days were full of activity, the nights were long and quiet and Padraic's absence was felt all night long.

I believed it would help to be with crowds of people, but it did not really help, because the Disney complex and all the other amusement parks were full of parents and their children and every time I saw a thirteen year old boy walking with his father I thought of Padraic.

One evening I was standing on a beach with Nora looking out at the surf when this man came by with two young sons. They were tossing a Frisbee to one another. I stared at the trio and I was thinking how lucky he was to have two sons. Then suddenly eight-year-old Nora very gently took my hand and looked up at me with an expression of infinite sadness. I was shocked by her expression, because clearly she was telling me that while Padraic was gone she was still there, and she needed my love and attention.

That incident was a turning point, because from moment on I decided to be supportive of Nora and help her through her grief, and I mourned Padraic in private and not in her presence.

At the end of two weeks I went back to work at the World Trade Center, where I was a marketing supervisor, and the first couple of days were the hardest of my life. Many of my coworkers had been at the wake and expressed their sympathy, but others had not and did not express any sympathy when I returned, because they did not know what to say to me.

The worst part was attending meetings with a score of people, because typically at these meetings people cracked jokes and talked in a light-hearted way, and my mind was frozen with grief and I could barely tolerate the laughter.

At one of these meetings there was a woman named Lois Bohovesky, who staged puppet shows at the World Trade Center every Christmas season. After the meeting was over Lois asked me to go with her and have a cup of coffee as there was something very important that she wanted to talk to me about. I went with her and when we were sitting in the restaurant she told me that I was in a state of shock—that she could see it in my eyes, and that I should take some advice that she was about to give me.

The advice was to join a group called Compassionate Friends, which was a support group for parents who had lost children.

"You really need to get involved with people who know how you feel; people who have been and still are in the boat you are in now. It is critical you get that support."

"Nobody in your office has a clue about the destructive nature of what has happened to you. They don't know how to talk to you. And many think it best not to bring up your loss at all because they think it will only upset you."

I listened to Lois because I knew she was well qualified to talk to me about losing a child violently. The previous year her sixteen-year-old daughter had been kidnapped on her way home from school, dragged into the woods, raped, and murdered. Lois knew all about horror, grief and the effects it has on the mind. She had become an expert at that.

Lois had very good advice to give to Eileen and I about how to go about coping with the tragedy and how to handle our relations with our friends and neighbors who had no idea about what we were going through.

"People expect you to mourn for a short period of time and then get over it. They believe that life goes on and they expect you to pick up the pieces as soon as possible. Most of them will never talk about Padraic again and will be very embarrassed if you bring his name up. They will think you are being very bad mannered if you try to share your grief with them. That, unfortunately, is human nature.

"And yet for a long time to come Padraic's death will be all that will be on your mind and you may be compelled to talk about him, no matter what others think of you.

"It is for this reason that you should join a local chapter of Compassionate Friends. Every member of the group has lost a child. When you are in the room with these people you will be with people who have lost children and not one of them will think you ill mannered to bring up your son's name, because they all do it.

"This a place where you can vent your feelings and can find comfort in the knowledge that you are not alone – that there are millions who are in the same boat as you are. But you will not find a cure for your sorrow there; you will just find some tools to cope with your sorrow.

"You may not like going to those meetings, and if this is the case do not go, they are not for everybody. But give it a try anyway. You have nothing to lose."

I took Lois Bohevesky's advice and for the next several years found a haven where I could talk about my loss with new friends from Compassionate Friends. Eileen came with me to a number of the meetings, but she was not comfortable venting her grief to relative strangers and preferred to talk to a few close friends instead. So, I would go alone.

Our approach to grieving was in many ways typical of married couples, because there is no right or wrong way to grieve and each individual has to find a way to handle the grief in a manner that is most comfortable.

Padraic's death drew Eileen closer to our Church, and for many years she read and cherished a copy of the *Good News Bible*, which Padraic had used at school. She also attended Mass not only on Sundays but on many weekdays as well.

Padraic's death did not change my religious views one way or the other. I remained a skeptic about all organized religion but I was not an atheist.

**THE GRANDCHILDREN
EILEEN AND JOSEPH FITZPATRICK**

In recent years, however, Eileen and I have been given what seems to be like a second chance.

Nora grew up to be a talented stable young woman in spite of the tragedy she experienced when she was eight, a tragedy that was catastrophic for her, because Padraic, who was five years older than her, always looked out for her. She went on to graduate from the University of Pennsylvania and while there met her husband Joseph Bernard Fitzpatrick 111.

In December 2003, eighteen years after Padraic's death she gave birth to a beautiful boy, Joseph Bernard Fitzpatrick 1V. The day he was born I felt a sense of renewal ... a sense that I had another chance to love a child ... and I could see my joy reflected in Eileen, who absolutely adores the little boy.

On August 21st, 2005, Nora gave birth to a beautiful little girl named Eileen Teresa Fitzpatrick, and our joy knew no bounds.

Neither of us sees Joseph and Eileen as replacements for Padraic because Padraic is irreplaceable. However, we both have learned by the arrival of our grandchildren that even after a great tragedy it is possible to find joy in life once again and enter into the type of relationship with children that make life worthwhile.

*   *   *